"Why this change of heart?"
Glenn asked

"Heather is their only grandchild, and their daughter's dead...."

"Perhaps that's why I'd rather she didn't go," Kira said with sudden fierceness.

Glenn was quick to interpret her meaning. "You're afraid they might want to keep her. Why on earth didn't you say this was at the back of your mind?"

"Because it sounds so damned selfish!"

A light that was almost amusement came into his eyes, and fury promptly flashed in her own.

"Damn you," she breathed savagely. "Don't you laugh at me!"

With predatory swiftness he caught hold of her wrist. "I'm not laughing at you. If I smiled, it was because you sounded so human."

JENNY ARDEN, a British writer, combines a career as a college lecturer in business studies with the writing she has always wanted to do. Her favorite place for relaxation is North Wales, but travel fascinates her—both the places she has visited and the places she dreams about for future journeying. In her spare time she enjoys sculpting historical figures in clay and cooking for company. Huckleberry, her Burmese Blue cat, is her companion while writing. He usually sits in a chair beside the typewriter, but occasionally, in a fit of jealousy, will bid for her attention by sitting on the keys!

Books by Jenny Arden

HARLEQUIN PRESENTS
1063—TO THE VICTOR, THE SPOILS

HARLEQUIN ROMANCE
2995—SOME ENCHANTING EVENING

Don't miss any of our special offers. Write to us at the following address for information on our newest releases.

Harlequin Reader Service
901 Fuhrmann Blvd., P.O. Box 1397, Buffalo, NY 14240
Canadian address: P.O. Box 603,
Fort Erie, Ont. L2A 5X3

JENNY ARDEN

friend or foe

Harlequin Books

TORONTO • NEW YORK • LONDON
AMSTERDAM • PARIS • SYDNEY • HAMBURG
STOCKHOLM • ATHENS • TOKYO • MILAN

For my mother

Harlequin Presents first edition November 1989
ISBN 0-373-11215-7

Original hardcover edition published in 1989
by Mills & Boon Limited

CHAPTER ONE

THE FLIGHT from Montpellier to London was nearly over. Kira glanced at Heather, her ten-year-old stepdaughter, who was gazing out of the window at the billowing cloud banks. A wave of unexpected gladness at the thought of being home caught hold of her. Despite the empty house that was waiting for them, London was where she and Heather belonged.

The six-month stay in Provence had been good for both of them. Heather seemed to have adjusted to her father's death of a year ago, while for Kira the complete change of scene had given her the space she'd so desperately needed to come to terms with the burden of grief and confusion. She supposed she should be grateful to Glenn Mason for giving her his permission to take Heather to France, but she still hated being in any way indebted to the man she had always considered to be her enemy.

Her fingers went to twist her wedding ring. She knew that Glenn had been perceptive enough to see the flaws in her marriage to his business partner and best friend. Quick to censure, doubtless he blamed her, too, for the accident in which Stuart had died. Pain tightened round her heart and her eyes began to smart, but she would not cry. For everything there is a season, she reminded herself fiercely, and her time for weeping was over. Now she must make a new start, concentrate on providing Heather with a happy and stable home and, above all, try not to antagonise Glenn any more than she had done already.

The drone of the aircraft's engine altered in pitch

and Heather turned to her to say excitedly, 'We must be nearly there now.'

'Yes, we'll be landing at Heathrow in a few minutes,' Kira said, adding with an affectionate smile, 'You're glad to be back, aren't you?'

'France was nice,' Heather answered. 'But it feels as if we've been away for ever, and I can't wait to see Uncle Glenn again. He will be at the airport to meet us, won't he?'

'You know Uncle Glenn,' Kira said lightly, masking her animosity towards Heather's guardian. 'He never breaks his promises.'

The seat-belt lights flashed on. The large plane started to shudder as it began its final descent. From out of the window the tiny houses grew larger, the fields greener, and then, with a jolt, the plane touched down on the runway, the screaming engines changing to a muted throb as it taxied into position.

'We're home!' Heather breathed.

Kira laughed and started to collect up their belongings, including the bottle of fine malt whisky she'd bought for Glenn. A peace offering, she thought wryly.

She knew he would see a change in her appearance and she was glad of it. The weeks in hospital following the car crash had left her like a wraith. Physically she had eventually made a good recovery. Emotionally the wounds had remained unhealed and, despite the brave act she'd put on, strain had been visible in her taut face.

Now, having regained weight, she was slim and supple in the pleat-front trousers and shapely waisted jumper she'd chosen to travel in. She didn't tan easily, but her fair skin was as lovely as porcelain and was set off by her bright chestnut hair that fell around her shoulders. Once again her eyes seemed to have warm lights of their own, even if in their amber depths they held a sadness she was unaware of. Glenn could no longer say with any justification that she wasn't strong enough to be taking care of Heather.

She followed her stepdaughter along the aisle to join the queue of disembarking passengers. A gust of air swept in where the exit opened on to the enclosed walkway, bracing after the somnolent warmth of the aircraft. It was early April and the weather was blustery and spring-like.

As they came through Passport Control Heather let go of her hand and ran ahead to the carousel where she quickly spotted their Burberry luggage. They were channelled through Customs with the same efficiency to emerge in the vast Arrivals Hall.

Kira was surprised how good it was to be back among everything that was familiar, to hear English voices among the babel of noise. It was only the thought of seeing Glenn again that dampened her sense of home-coming. Yet outwardly she seemed quite at ease as, with Heather at her side, she halted with their luggage trolley to scan the crush of people who were waiting to meet friends and relations.

She caught sight of Glenn at the same time that Heather shrilled, 'There's Uncle Glenn!'

He was heading straight for them, the people in his path automatically moving aside for the man who had all the arrogant grace of a tiger. Immediately Kira felt a prickle of hostility run up her spine. Even his walk seemed to put her on the defensive. It was so obviously that of a man used to coming on the scene to take charge and to set things straight.

He must have come direct from the City, for he was wearing a grey business suit that should have tempered his driving masculinity but which, instead, made him convey an unsettling impression of urbanity and danger. Kira, her eyes guarded, watched him approach. She'd never found it easy to be spontaneous with him at the best of times. Now, remembering the furious scene they'd had before she and Heather had left for Provence, she was certain she'd never manage to be natural with him again.

Heather darted forward, running up to him to be hugged. Glenn smiled as he swung the little girl effortlessly off her feet. The genuine warm smile in his strong, attractive face made Kira glance away. Glenn's firm mouth had a hint of sensuality and, frequently, of humour. Yet when he spoke to her his face was generally as hard as a fist. Though the feeling was mutual, it still antagonised her to know how much he disliked her.

'It's good to see you, mischief,' he said, giving Heather's ponytail a little teasing tug as he released her.

'And you,' Heather answered, smiling up at him. She tucked her hand in his and went on happily, 'We missed you.'

Kira caught the faintly sardonic look he flashed her. Heather spoke solely for herself and, after the words Kira had flung at him, he could have little doubt of it. But his resolute voice was surprisingly friendly as he said, 'Hello, Kira. Welcome home.'

Putting a casual hand on her shoulder, he bent to kiss her. It was no more than a brush of his lips against her cheek, but it was so completely unexpected that she caught her breath. Though Glenn was long on charm, the only time he'd ever kissed her before had been when he'd wished her well on her wedding day. He'd seemed to have as strong a wish to keep her at arm's length as she had to avoid any form of physical contact between them.

She flashed him a glance from under her long lashes. Her pulse had quickened quite alarmingly and she hoped he hadn't sensed it. From the first Glenn had made his opinion of her quite clear, and that alone had always made her immune to his masculine charisma.

But she could see why other women succumbed. The thought was strangely disturbing, arousing in her the strong desire to renew hostilities with him.

Determinedly she brought the impulse under control as he took the trolley from her and asked, 'Did you have a good flight?'

'Everything went very smoothly,' she answered, forcing herself to smile.

'I suppose your father saw you off?' Glenn enquired as they made their way towards the automatic sliding doors.

'Yes. He and Fabienne drove us to the airport. They waited with us till our flight was called.'

'They've got a lovely house, Uncle Glenn,' Heather put in, 'with figs and grapes in the conservatory. It was just beautiful and the swimming pool was super.'

The little girl wanted to tell him in detail about their stay with Kira's father and his wife. Kira was glad of her chatter. Despite the help Glenn was giving her, she was finding it hard to make small talk with him.

His silver-grey Mercedes was parked in the short-stay car park. The accident had made Kira nervous even as a passenger, but worse than that was the sudden fear that they would drive along the dual carriageway where the accident had happened.

Her heart began to thud sickeningly. She wanted to ask Glenn to take a different route, but her voice wouldn't come. She struggled to bring her emotions in check. Her thoughts were of Heather. The little girl hadn't been in the car at the time of the accident, and the roads they took and the stretch of dual carriageway would have no significance for her. Kira intended it to remain that way. She mustn't say anything.

'I'm afraid we're going to hit the rush-hour traffic,' Glenn commented as they pulled out on to the road.

'It was very good of you to pick us up,' she said, icy remoteness disguising the chaos and panic inside her.

Glenn slanted a glance at her, his dark brows drawn together. Damn it, she thought, she hadn't meant to sound so hostile. Doubtless it would earn her some sarcastic reply in return.

Her hands were laced together tightly in her lap, the knuckles almost white. She didn't realise that, to a man as sharply observant as Glenn, they both explained and excused her behaviour. As though her hostility hadn't registered with him, he said conversationally, 'I thought we'd drive back through West Drayton. It should be quicker that way at this time of the evening.'

Immediately relief swamped her. She didn't know whether Glenn had made the decision solely because of the traffic or partly out of consideration to her, but whichever was the case she was profoundly grateful.

Heather, unaware of any hidden nuances, leaned forward to put an arm on the back of Kira's seat.

'Can I put my posters up in my room as soon as we get home?' she asked.

'You can have a free hand with them,' Kira promised.

'Except that you're not going home tonight, sweetheart,' Glenn said easily. 'You can put them up tomorrow.'

'What do you mean, not going home?' Kira asked.

'I mean you're staying the night at my place.'

'*Are* we?' Heather asked eagerly.

'No, I don't know that we are,' Kira said, challenged by the way Glenn had of taking control.

He raised a competent hand briefly off the wheel as he said, more kindness in his voice than she was used to from him, 'I know your house is only fifteen minutes or so away from where I live, but it's been empty for six months. It would be a pretty cheerless welcome for you on your return home. It makes much better sense for you to stay with me tonight and to settle in tomorrow.'

She saw that she could hardly refuse without sounding ungracious, and anyway the atmosphere between them was so much better than she had expected that she was ready to be amenable.

'In which case, thank you. It's very kind of you,' she said.

'Will Mrs Bradshaw be there?' Heather piped in.

'Yes, she's got your room ready.'

'She's nice,' Heather commented.'

'I agree,' Glenn answered, his eyes crinkling, 'which means I'm sorry she's retiring soon. Housekeepers like her are hard to replace.'

'You could always get married instead,' Heather suggested. 'A wife would look after you even better than Mrs Bradshaw.'

'I'll bear it in mind,' he said, obviously amused by the little girl.

Kira smiled, and realised to her surprise that she was beginning to relax.

'So when are you starting work at the hospital?' Glenn asked her.

'Next week.'

'That's very soon,' he commented.

'I want to get back,' she answered, adding quickly, 'I'll be working the same hours as I was before. It won't interfere with my looking after Heather.'

'I didn't say it would,' Glenn said with just a touch of impatience.

'I . . . I thought you didn't like my working.'

'You're very quick to make judgements about me, aren't you?'

'I thought *you* were about *me*,' she retaliated.

Amusement touched the corners of his mouth.

'It turns out it's no generalisation that redheads are quick-tempered,' he remarked.

He had never teased her before, and there was something about the tone of his voice that made her laugh in spite of herself.

'I happen to be the exception that proves the rule,'

she said. 'It's just that . . .'

She broke off. She'd hardly get a prize for tact for saying that he brought out the worst in her. She fell silent, and the wayward instant of rapport with him vanished as quickly as it had come.

Glenn rekindled the conversation by saying, 'Did you have much social life in France?'

If she hadn't known him so well she wouldn't have detected that his well-pitched voice was a shade clipped. Glenn was a master at concealing his annoyance. Always the impression he gave was one of controlled energy, of a man who was both purposeful and inscrutable.

But just the same she took the lead he had given her. If she couldn't master her antipathy towards him, at the very least she could mask it. For a while the conversation continued naturally as if they were old friends. No outsider would have guessed at the undercurrent between them, of a hidden telepathy of thought and contention.

Heather, who had been very talkative at first, had now fallen asleep, lulled by the steady speed of the Mercedes. Kira glanced over her shoulder at the little girl and commented with a smile, 'I thought she'd gone very quiet. The journey must have tired her. She's fast asleep.'

She turned back and, as she did so, a Volvo approaching the main road from a side-turning braked sharply on the double white line. Kira gasped and flinched instinctively, realising too late that there was no danger. Her hands were trembling and her face pale as she said to Glenn, 'I'm . . . I'm sorry. For a minute I thought we were going to be hit in the side.'

She sensed his eyes on her and bit her lip. She felt self-conscious and far too easy to read.

'I'd no idea you were still so nervy in a car,' he said.

She mistook the quiet ferocity in his voice for

intolerance, and lashed out angrily, 'I'm not!'

'We won't argue about it,' he said with dry firmness.

She looked down, far more shaken than she wanted Glenn to see. Unexpectedly he reached for her hand, covering it with his own. She couldn't speak without giving away her emotion, but she put up a silent resistance, clenching her fingers into her palm. She wasn't used to his touching her, and she assumed it was that which explained the static that flickered along her nerves.

'Just relax,' he said gently. 'You're perfectly safe.'

'You don't have to take it as a slur on your ability at the wheel,' she answered stormily, wanting no compassion from the man who had always treated her with a chivalry that was more cold and formal than outright contempt would have been.

'Are you as antagonistic with everyone as you are with me?' he asked with a touch of sarcasm. 'Or am I privileged with special treatment?'

He released her hand and with dismay she realised she was behaving with him not at all as she'd intended. She said in a cramped voice. 'I'm sorry.'

'That's the second time you've apologised to me in the last two minutes,' he said curtly, before ordering, 'Stop it, Kira.'

She didn't answer, and there was a short pause before he said, his tone more lenient, 'You know, the best way for you to get over the accident would be for you to start driving again.'

Even the thought of it made her mouth go dry. The accident had been caused by a van careering across a dual carriageway. She had been completely exonerated, but despite that she couldn't forget that she had passed her driving test not two weeks previously and, more especially, that she had argued with Stuart over which of them should drive to the airport that day. If he had been at the wheel of the Jaguar, might he have been able to swerve in time?

'I will drive again,' she answered defensively. 'When I'm ready.'

'You're not the type to run away from something just because it scares you.'

It was so rare for him to suggest he found anything praiseworthy in her character that it confused her, especially in this instance, because she was certain she didn't merit his confidence. He went on, 'But the longer you leave it, the harder it's going to be. It's a year now since the crash.'

Threatened by the undertone of authority in his voice, she said, 'It may have been a year. But I'm still not ready to drive. In any case, it's *my* decision.'

'Only you're not going to make that decision without a bit of gentle pushing from time to time.'

'Not from you, Glenn,' she said warningly. 'Stuart gave you the right to interfere in Heather's life, not mine.'

'So we're back to that again!'

'Look, can't we just leave the topic of my driving alone?' she asked, angry not only with him but with herself. Why had she let him provoke her into voicing a resentment she'd sworn that in future she'd keep silent about?

'I'm a friend, Kira,' he answered curtly. 'That gives me the right to be concerned about you.'

'A friend?' she queried sceptically, unable to stop herself. 'You were a friend of my husband's.'

'But never of yours,' he completed the sentence for her, his jawline tight. 'Well, perhaps not. But things are different now.'

'In what way?' she challenged.

'For one, because we've had a spell apart. For another, this time I intend we make a start with getting to know each other.'

'We've known each other for five years!'

'*Have* we? I was Stuart's business partner and you were his wife. Neither of us looked any deeper than that to see what else we might have in common. But perhaps now's the time to try it.'

In her own mind she was convinced that any such attempt would be futile. The best she could ever hope for in her relationship with Glenn was a kind of armed truce. But, trying to meet him half-way, she said, 'Well, I'm game if you are.'

The car was gliding effortlessly up the steep incline of Roxeth Hill when Heather woke up, stretched and exclaimed in surprise, 'We're almost there!'

'You've slept nearly the whole way,' Kira smiled.

At the top of the hill the Mercedes turned into the High Street, past the sixteenth century white-fronted King's Head Hotel and the few select shops with their quaint bow-fronted windows. Boys from Harrow School were strolling along the twisted street in the evening sunlight, books under their arms. The trees that clustered on the slopes were coming into leaf. Kira, who had always loved the timeless charm of the Hill, gave a soft sigh.

Glenn glanced at her and quoted lightly, ' "Oh, to be in England, now that April's there." '

'How did you know . . .?' she began sharply, breaking off and adding with a breath of slightly wary laughter, 'That's exactly what I was thinking.'

'Lucky guess,' Glenn commented with his charismatic smile.

He turned in under a carriage archway, and brought the Mercedes to a halt on the gravelled drive outside the house. With its porticoed entrance and long, symmetrical sash windows, it had all the elegance and simplicity that belonged to the Regency age. Well-tended borders beyond the drive gave way to lawns which sloped down in a series of terraces to a carpet of early daffodils and narcissi. The house, which wouldn't have been out of place on the front cover of *Homes and Gardens*, represented a very sound investment, something Stuart, with his highly competitive instincts, had been mildly jealous of.

Mrs Bradshaw, Glenn's housekeeper, came to the front door on hearing the car draw up outside.

'Good evening, Mrs Newall,' she began in her friendly North Country voice, before smiling, 'Hello, Heather. I've put you in the little blue room at the end of the landing on the second floor.'

'Has it got a a dormer window?' Heather asked hopefully.

'I thought that would be what you'd choose,' Mrs Bradshaw laughed. 'Yes, it's got a dormer window and the views are lovely. On a very clear day you can even see the Post Office Tower in the distance.'

After the journey, Kira was ready for the cup of tea Mrs Bradshaw suggested. Assured by the housekeeper that Heather wouldn't get under her feet, she allowed the little girl to go back with her into the kitchen. Now, for the first time since her return, she was alone with Glenn. She hunted for something inconsequential to say, disliking the strange constraint she felt in his presence even now that the mood was more relaxed between them. Instead, he spoke first.

'I thought you and I would eat out this evening,' he said. 'There are a couple of things we ought to sort out.'

Immediately suspicion flashed into her eyes.

'What things?' she asked carefully.

'Let's not pre-empt the discussion now,' Glenn answered. 'We'll talk over dinner. I've booked a table at the Apollo for eight o'clock. I think you'll like it there.'

Though she gave no sign of it, her mistrust of him flared. What did he want to talk to her about? It had to concern Heather. Ever since Kira had learned that Stuart had appointed Glenn as his daughter's guardian she had been afraid that he might take the little girl away from her. He had never thought well of her, and that was before the explosive row she'd had with him six months ago!

He carried the suitcases upstairs and left her to change. She glanced about the room, her expression troubled. A Japanese-style flower arrangement had been placed thoughtfully on the white dressing-table. Its assorted shades of apricot harmonised with the attractive colour scheme. The double bed was centrally placed, surrounded by an expanse of thick-piled carpet that felt luxuriously soft as she kicked her shoes off.

If only she had insisted that Glenn drive her and Heather straight home. Then there could have been no ominous sounding discussion with him. But if he was going to suggest making alternative arrangements concerning Heather's care she would fight him with every weapon in her armoury, no matter what her position was legally.

Not for the first time she felt a stir of hot anger at the difficult situation she was in. Heather had been five when she had married Stuart, and since that time Kira had become like a mother to her. From the start Heather had accepted her without any problems. Doubtless it had helped that she had worked with the little girl for three months for therapy with a stammer, which was how she and Stuart had met. With a natural way with children, Kira loved her as dearly as if she was her own, and yet she now had no rights whatsoever regarding her upbringing. She was dependent entirely on Glenn's magnanimity and goodwill.

While she'd been in Provence she'd made a real mental effort to come to terms with the fact that Heather was his ward. And possibly if Stuart had appointed anyone else she could have accepted his decision, but she and Glenn were long-term enemies.

She went into the bathroom and began to shower.

As the warm jets streamed, soothing and refreshing, over her skin, her thoughts stayed focused on Glenn. Right from the first time she had met him there had been antagonism between them.

She and Stuart had celebrated their engagement very quietly, and it wasn't till a short while later that she'd been introduced to him. He was a senior partner in the firm of accountants Stuart had established, and he'd been away on business when they'd announced their engagement. Stuart had wanted him to be best man and Glenn had asked them both out to dinner.

She had already heard quite a bit about him. She knew that he and Stuart had attended the same school, though Stuart had been higher up, being some six years older. For a time Stuart had dated one of Glenn's sisters, but Kira wasn't sure how serious the relationship had been. Later, when Glenn was a qualified chartered accountant, advising the merchant banks on new share issues, Stuart had determinedly set out to persuade him to join his firm. Glenn had held out for the most ruthlessly advantageous terms, and Stuart had finally conceded to them. He wanted a specialist on corporate tax and Glenn was an expert, with the steadiness of purpose and razor-sharp mind that made him a particularly valuable asset to the firm.

From what Stuart had told her, Kira had formed a mental picture of what he would be like. She knew he had three sisters and that family was important to him. She expected to meet a tall, rather intense man, bookish rather than athletic, astuteness hiding behind a certain diffidence.

When Stuart had introduced them that image had been abruptly shattered. Glenn was tall, certainly, but lean and powerful with it. Darkly good-looking, he had an unnervingly direct gaze and a quiet, urbane manner that gave rise to a disturbing feeling of hidden possibilities. And, added to that, he was very at ease with women.

It was curious how vividly she could remember that initial meeting. He had taken the hand she had offered him in a firm grasp, while his vivid blue eyes held hers.

'It's good to meet you, Kira,' he said, with a smile that didn't soften the hard, attractive lines of his face. 'Stuart's a very lucky man.'

His voice was firm and well-pitched, but his eyes were coldly appraising and immediately she felt defensive. He was judging her, acknowledging that she was striking to look at with her Titian colouring. But he plainly had reservations about her and he didn't mind that she sensed it. With a flash of hostility she wondered if he had doubts about her motives for marrying at twenty-four, when they had known each other for so short a time, a man who was not only extremely well-off, but also thirteen years her senior.

But Glenn was Stuart's friend and business partner. She couldn't let it show that they hadn't clicked. And in any case she hoped that with time perhaps they would warm to each other. But that hadn't happened. Instead, despite the pretence of accord between them, the enmity had become fiercer.

Stuart liked to entertain and frequently asked her to organise a dinner party for influential clients. He didn't seem to mind if on occasions they were over-attentive to her. But some instinct would warn her of Glenn's iron-hard gaze. Glancing defiantly in his direction, she would see that his face was tautly expressionless and that contempt smouldered in the depths of his dark blue eyes. With no option but to be gracious to her husband's guests, it infuriated her to realise that Glenn saw her as a brittle little flirt.

But, if he was an expert at scrupulous courtesy, she soon proved she was his equal. For Stuart's sake she matched politeness with politeness and, on the surface at least, tried to get along with Glenn. And to her credit she had succeeded quite faultlessly—until six months ago.

She stepped out of the shower, wrapping one of the fluffy white towels around her, sarong-fashion. She still deeply regretted the furious row she'd had with him. The words she'd said then could not now be taken back, and, completely in his power, she'd been an utter fool to express her hatred of him so clearly.

She slippped on her ivory silk undies, debating what to wear in view of the fact that she was anticipating trouble. Her jersey two-piece was probably the best choice. In delicately patterned almond green, with a fluted skirt and a deceptively simple top, it made her look engagingly slim and spirited. Just knowing that would help her stand up to him if need be.

Catching sight of herself in the mirror, she paused, staring for a moment with unfathomable eyes at the scars on her right shoulder and upper chest. Her pretty camisole, with its soft silk sheen and deep inset of lace, somehow made the disfiguring marks more cruel. She traced the worst of them with her fingers before briskly reaching for her top. She tried the jabot so that the effect was carefully careless and secured it with a citrine pin. The scars were ugly, but she was lucky to be alive and the only thing to do about them was to be sensible.

She went downstairs to find Heather and Mrs Bradshaw playing draughts in the drawing-room. The log fire was now lit in the marble fireplace and it burned with the faint, inviting fragrance of pine. It was impossible not to feel at home in the room.

Kira liked the oriental carpet with its deep, bold colours, and the solid antique furniture. On the walls was an interesting choice of pictures, ranging from Chagall prints to modern originals. Faint puzzlement came into her eyes. It was strange, she thought, that she should so like his taste when, on a personal level, she and Glenn seemed poles apart. His voice in the car

came back to her. How well *did* she know this man she
was possibly about to cross swords with yet again?'

CHAPTER TWO

KIRA joined Heather on the sofa to see how the game was progressing.

'There, look at that!' Mrs Bradshaw exclaimed laughingly as Heather jumped her black counter over two white ones and removed them from the board.

'I've been practising with Kira,' she stated with a touch of pride.

Glenn's resonant voice came from the doorway.

'Is she any good?'

There was a faint shading of amusement in his tone and, as he advanced into the room, Kira's eyes stayed on him as she tried to monitor his mood. Heather nodded and said, 'Yes, but she keeps her kings in the back row and you say you should always use them to attack.'

'Perhaps she likes to play safe.'

Ready to rise to any challenge from him, real or perceived, Kira answered, 'I'd rather play safe than get my fingers burned.'

'That's a cautious philosophy.'

This time there was no mistaking the inflection of humour and for an instant she was almost tempted to tease him back, Except she didn't dare. Her distrust of him went too deep.

The restaurant he drove them to had a warm, friendly ambience. It was one she hadn't been to before, and she was puzzled by his choice. Candlelight played on the pristine white tablecloths, and against the background of bouzouki music there was the babel of talk and laughter. This was a place to relax and unwind, not a setting for a cold verbal fencing match.

She picked up the menu and commented, 'I wouldn't have thought somewhere like this was quite your scene.'

'Is that why I keep getting such wary glances from you?'

She coloured slightly and replied, 'You said we had things to discuss. Of course I'm curious to know why you've asked me here.'

'In part, as I expect you've guessed, I want to talk to you about Heather.'

She felt herself go cold. How right she had been to suspect him! She clenched her hands under the table, but her voice was perfectly even as she said defiantly 'You don't approve of the way I'm looking after her?'

Glenn drew his hawkish brows together.

'And whatever gave you that idea?' he asked. 'You're doing an excellent job and you must know it.'

Steeled for the worst, she couldn't immediately hide her relief, and his blue eyes narrowed on her.

'Exactly what were you expecting me to say?'

'With you, I never know what to expect.'

'Evidently,' he replied crisply. 'But just what makes you think I'm not perfectly satisfied with the way you're taking care of Heather?'

Kira hesitated, and then, dropping her gaze, said awkwardly, 'I . . . I said a lot of things to you six months ago. I know I acted in a very high-strung way . . .'

'And because of it you jumped to the conclusions that I'd decide Heather would be better off being looked after by someone else,' Glenn finished the sentence for her shortly. Rather more gently, he went on, 'I haven't got you labelled as some kind of neurotic because of one argument between us. I realise the strain you'd been under. *You* were the only person who seemed to think you had to carry on so valiantly all the time.'

To describe the exchange as an argument was far too

mild. He had called round at her house to tell her he intended to arrange for Heather to visit her maternal grandparents in Toronto. Kira had immediately voiced her opposition and in doing so all her pent-up grief and antagonism had suddenly exploded to the surface. She was certain that her torrent of angry words and distraught tears had shocked Glenn as much as, afterwards, they had her. It was the only explanation she could find for his sudden generosity in allowing her to take Heather to Provence.

'Just the same,' she said, 'I shouldn't have lost my temper the way I did.'

'Forget it,' Glenn ordered quietly. 'I have. Now, are you ready to order?'

At that moment she almost liked him. His whole attitude had been far more understanding than she had expected. No longer feeling on trial, she started to talk to him more naturally, accepting that he had a right to ask about the school his ward had attended in France and the progress she'd made there.

The evening went quickly. Considering the cold, stilted conversations they'd had in the past, it was surprising how easily they moved on from one topic to another. Glenn was stimulating company and, although once or twice they veered towards fencing, somehow he seemed to retrieve the relaxed mood and they ended up in a joking clash.

They were lingering over coffee when he said, 'While you were away, did you think any more about Heather's trip to Canada?'

'So that's what this evening's been about!' she said sharply.

'I take it that means you're still against the idea,' he said with dry understatement.

She deliberately gave herself time before answering, determined she would not over-react with him on this topic twice.

'No,' she replied. 'I'm not against it. I just think it's too soon.'

'Don't stonewall me, Kira. I want your reasons. Last autumn you were completely run down. I felt you needed a break from taking care of Heather, her grandparents very much wanted to see her. The trip seemed a good idea all round. But you were violently against it. I didn't push you for your reasons then, but I intend knowing them now.'

'Why?' she demanded. 'Will it make any difference *what* I think? After all, as you pointed out, *my* consent isn't needed.'

'Perhaps we both said more than we should have that night,' he said, the curbed force to his words giving way to faint sarcasm as he continued, 'I hoped that a break from seeing one another would give you the chance to get over your resentment towards me. It seems I was over-optimistic.'

'I don't resent you,' she corrected him, trying hard to mean it. 'I admit, initially I found Stuart's decision difficult to accept, but I wasn't expected to pull through after the crash. I understand why he appointed you as Heather's guardian.'

It was ironic that, when on admittance to hospital she'd lapsed almost immediately into a coma, she'd been the one to survive. Stuart, who'd never been on the danger list, had died suddenly three days afterwards. She wondered if he'd had some strange presentiment of death that he'd insisted Glenn put his affairs so much in order for him. Or perhaps his protectiveness towards his young daughter had made him determined to guard against the worst.

She went on, her voice subdued, 'I don't mean to be unreasonable over this. I . . . I suppose I'm thinking of what Stuart wanted.'

She knew that was a lie even as she said it. One of the first disagreements between her and Stuart had centred on the issue she and Glenn were discussing now. A card had come from Heather's grandparents for her sixth birthday and Stuart had promptly torn it up.

Kira had been both startled and indignant. Heather had no grandparents on her father's side. Stuart was deliberately cutting her off from an important relationship. She'd pointed this out to him, but he'd immediately blown up, reminding her that Heather was his daughter.

What had upset Kira was that this was apparently his way of making his first wife's parents pay for helping her to try to win custody of Heather. Kira hated that sort of bitterness, and it was doubly cruel as Kathryn had been drowned in a sailing accident while the divorce was in progress and the battle for custody was still being fought. Now, obviously, Heather was more than ever important to her grandparents.

On several occasions Kira had tried to persuade him to relent. But it had been useless. Each subsequent birthday and Christmas card had been torn up without Heather ever having seen them.

Glenn's voice broke into her thoughts.

'When I first contacted Heather's grandparents a year ago, you seemed pleased,' he reminded her. 'In fact, you encourgaed Heather to write back. So why this change of heart now? She's their only grandchild and their daughter's dead . . .'

'Perhaps that's why I'd rather she didn't go,' Kira said with sudden fierceness.

Glenn was quick to interpret her meaning.

'You're afraid they might want to keep her,' he stated. 'Why on earth didn't you say this was at the back of your mind?'

'Because it sounds so damned selfish!'

A light that was almost amusement came into his eyes, and fury promptly flashed in her own. He had forced this confessesion out of her and now he found her reaction funny!'

'Damn you, she breathed savagely. 'Don't you laugh at me!'

With predatory swiftness he caught hold of her wrist, his firm grip emphasing his words as he said, 'I'm *not* laughing at you. If I smiled it was because you sounded so human.'

His voice, quiet, yet deliberate, held her arrested. She stared back into his eyes, the intensity of the moment such that, when he released her, she felt a shock go through her, almost as though she had broken away from some powerful magnetism.

Disturbed by the sensation, she flared, 'By human, do you mean irrational?'

'Irrational enough to keep me guessing,' he drawled.

Disliking his lazy tone, she snapped, 'Guessing about what?'

'What do men usually guess about women?'

Anger and shock at his audacity made her heartbeat quicken. With as much stony coldness as she could muster she said, 'I *beg* your pardon?'

'You don't have to drop the temperature to zero,' he jeered sardonically. 'I wasn't making a pass at you.'

She had been so certain of her ground, but with his dismissive mockery he'd swept it from under her. She felt herself colour, and in an attempt to recover her poise managed, 'I . . . I didn't think you were.'

'You're not a very good liar, Kira. Or did you *want* me to make a pass at you?'

'You insufferable egotist!' she breathed as she threw her napkin on the table.

Too quick for her to evade him, his hand closed on her wrist like a vice. 'You're not the sort to make a scene in public,' he said. 'But try and walk out on me and that's exactly what you'll do.'

His voice hardly altered in register, and it scarcely seemed to carry a warning in its pleasant conversational tone. But his eyes that stared her down were implacable. As always they were the real indication of the worth of the man. They were hard, piercing and dangerous and, not daring to defy him, she said in a mutinous undertone, 'Let go of my wrist!'

Instead of complying, his gaze taunted her as his strong, tanned hand slipped down over her knuckles. He turned her palm over, caressing it indolently with his thumb. Static jumped along her nerves in reflex response, making her eyes smoulder darkly.

'Amazing, isn't it?' Glenn said, his voice low and mocking, 'how you and I always manage to create a false impression. Right now, doubtless the motherly-looking woman who's watching us thinks we're lovers about to leave the restaurant to round off the evening in the most satisfactory of ways.'

'If there's one thing we'll never be, it's lovers,' she said in a hissing undertone.

'Then why not lower your guard with me for a change?' he demanded. 'I've already assured you it's perfectly safe for you to do so.'

'I might be able to, *if* you'd let go of me.'

With a faint, sardonic quirk of his brow he released her. Immediately she flexed her fingers, not because his grip had been the least bit crushing, but because he had dared to caress her and she refused to allow any memory of that to stay with her senses.

'What's wrong?' he asked softly. 'Don't you like being touched?'

Furiously she realised that the sensual note in his voice caused the same warm shiver to trace over her skin as when he touched her. Mutinously, she didn't answer and he went on, 'A year's a long time without any physical closeness . . .'

'I don't need *you* to satisfy any longings of that nature,' she cut across him angrily.

'You mean they're satisfied elsewhere?'

'I don't have to answer that! In fact, how dare you question me about my . . .'

She broke off stormily, and he supplied, his voice, as hard as his eyes, 'Lovers?'

She wanted to snap that she had no lovers, nor in the lonely year that Stuart had been dead any needs of the kind he had implied. Slow-burning resentment overcame the impulse.

'I am not going to discuss my sex-life with you,' she said coldly, though her eyes were dark and hot.

'You'll discuss anything with me that I damn well please,' he said.

She realised suddenly that, as her life affected Heather's, if he wanted he could force the issue. Why did she invariably over-react with him, making every situation worse? He probably assumed now that she had actually taken a lover while she'd been in France.

It rankled, but she was about to swallow her stiff pride and correct the impression she'd give him when he switched the conversation back to Kathryn's parents, and her chance was lost. Despite the fact that he'd been patient with her fears about her step-daughter's visit to Canada, she found her voice was cool as she agreed to his plans. She couldn't understand how, when the evening had been going so well, an angry clash had developed from out of nowhere. Tranquillity between them, even when she was trying her hardest, seemed impossible to attain.

They left the restaurant and arrived back at his house. Mrs Bradshaw and Heather had already gone to bed, and the fire in the drawing-room had burned low in the grate.

'Can I pour you a nightcap?' Glenn asked.

After the discord between them earlier, she knew it would look pointed if she refused.

'Thanks,' she answered.

'What will you have?'

'I'd like a green Chartreuse,' she said as she sat down in the armchair by the fire.

She watched him as he went over to the drinks cabinet. Even now that they were no longer warring, his pantherish tread made her feel on the alert. Everything about him, from his hard, mature body to his forceful personality, contrived in some strange way to unsettle her.

'I expected you to ask for a Tia Maria,' he commented.

'Am I that predictable?' she asked, and was slightly surprised by her spontaneity.

'On the contrary,' Glenn answered. 'You're one of the least predictable women I know. Perhaps that's what makes you interesting.'

She took the glass he handed her, careful to prevent her fingers from touching his.

'I hope that's a compliment,' she said, a flash of wariness in her eyes.

'What else?' he mocked as he sat down opposite her.

It was curious the way they could communicate at times with the very minimum of words. She knew perfectly that he was taunting her gently about the enmity between them in the past, making her smile wryly in response.

They talked for a while longer before he remarked, 'By the way, I meant to tell you, the institute's dinner is in three weeks' time. I know the subject must be painful but I'll need to know as soon as possible whether you intend to present the memorial prize yourself.'

Her heart contracted and it took her a moment to say, 'Yes, I'll present it myself.' Her voice sounded husky but she made herself add, 'Because of that row we had, I never got round to thanking you for setting up the trust fund. The idea of an annual award would have pleased Stuart very much.'

She saw Glenn frown. His hard gaze impaled her as

he replied levelly, 'It keeps his name alive, which is what you wanted.'

Hostility stiffened her spine. She knew the rapier thrust of those blue eyes and that slightly clipped edge to his words of old. Was it going through his mind that instead of arranging for a memorial prize she would have done better to have made Stuart happier while he was alive? If so, it was enough that she tortured *herself* with the thought.

She would always feel responsible that in the last year of Stuart's life their marriage had been under pressure. She had wanted a baby and she became increasingly impatient with his desire to wait. Frequently she felt that Heather was all the family he needed, despite his assurances that he shared her wish for children of their own.

They had started to argue. She couldn't seem to leave the topic alone and, when finally Stuart had agreed, it had been grudgingly. Looking back, she supposed that if she had conceived easily, the spark of tension would have been put out. But instead, as each month passed and she didn't become pregnant, she became increasingly trapped in an emotional web of frustration and disappointment. Knowing that Stuart didn't share her feelings, she couldn't talk about them openly, which might have brought them closer instead of acting as a barrier between them. Irritated by her uncharacteristic edginess, he had quickly become impatient. His brusque taunt came into her mind.

'Kathryn and I never planned to have Heather. Even taking precautions didn't stop *her* from becoming pregnant. If you can't conceive, there must be something wrong with you.'

There had been other equally insensitive remarks. She'd tried to ease the hurt of them by telling herself he hadn't meant to be cruel any more than she had meant the words she had flung at him in reply.

Until that last year Kira had never felt any jealousy over his first wife. From what Stuart had told her, his marriage to Kathryn had been stormy. Apparently she had been unreasonable and possessive. Finally she'd met someone else and had pressed for a divorce. Everything he'd told her had made Kira assume he had stopped loving Kathryn a long while back. It was his frequent references to her while they were trying for a baby that made her no longer so certain. Deep down she began desperately to need reassurance from him, and her failure to conceive made it all the more important for her to know Stuart still loved her.

If she hadn't been under such emotional pressure, perhaps the argument the morning of the crash wouldn't have flared. Stuart was flying to Jersey on a business trip. They had talked about her going with him as Heather was away on a school holiday in Bath, but Stuart had said she'd find it dull as he'd be in meetings most of the time. His flight was at eight-thirty, meaning he had to be up early. He'd been working long hours of late and had got home the previous evening at gone nine o'clock.

Needing to be close to him, and very much in tune with her monthly cycle, Kira had wanted to make love, but Stuart had said he was tired and not in the mood. He'd rejected her loving enticement almost crossly, and afterwards she'd lain awake beside him for a long time, close to tears of hurt and isolation, while he slept.

In the morning, over breakfast, he'd made an attempt to make up, but Kira had impatiently pushed his arms away. When they were ready to leave, she picked up the car keys to his Jaguar from the hall table automatically.

'No, I'll drive,' Stuart said.

'I'm going to drive back from the airport once I've dropped you,' she pointed out, 'so I may as well drive both ways.'

'I don't like being driven,' he answered, as though that ended the discussion.

'Or do you mean you don't like being driven by a woman?' she asked.

'For God's sake, don't be so damned childish!'

'I don't think I am being childish,' she retaliated. 'I'd have started driving much sooner if you hadn't always been so chauvinistic about it.'

'OK, so I think men make better drivers than women, but I'm not alone in that opinion. Now, do we have to make an issue out of it?' Stuart said with an edge of irritation as he held out his hand for the keys.

But she did have to make an issue out of it. The heated row that developed wasn't really about who should do the driving. It was about his refusal to share with her the pressures of trying for a baby. And because the night before he had made her feel abandoned and rejected and vulnerable she was determined not to give in over driving to the airport.

Angrily he had allowed her to have her way, but though they'd talked with a pretence of civility during the drive, she had to live with the fact that he'd died without her having the chance to make up that final argument. Even now that her grief had dulled, she still had nightmares when she recalled the crash with horrific intensity. They snatched her awake, leaving her cold and shaken to replay in the empty hours of the night the memories of her marriage. Why had she had to mar the last year of Stuart's life with her longing for a baby she couldn't conceive and her jealousy over Kathryn?

She started as Glenn took her glass from her.

'Are you going to sleep on me?' he asked gently.

The remoteness left her eyes and, quickly coming back to the present, she said with the ghost of a laugh, 'I'm sorry. I was miles away. What were you saying?'

There was no way she was ever going to let Glenn

know about the regrets that haunted her.

'I was asking you what your plans are now that you're home,' he said as he leaned back in his chair.

Even the relaxed stillness of his lithe man's body antagonised her faintly. For all the improvement in accord between them this evening, had he really modified his opinion of her? She reminded herself that, whether he had or not, she had resolved to stop warring with him, and answered, 'This weekend I plan to get the house aired and to settle in. I also want to take Heather shopping. She needs some new school uniform for the summer term. And then, of course, on Tuesday I start work at the hospital.'

'I understand you want to keep busy,' Glenn said. 'But don't overdo things. Scars take time to fade.'

He meant the emotional trauma of the accident. Yet instinctively her hand went to the jabot she had tied at her throat. From Glenn, more than anyone, she didn't want pity.

'I won't overdo things,' she promised as she stood up to say goodnight.

He got to his feet also as he said, 'No, I intend seeing that you don't.'

His words held a note of male authority, and she found herself replaying them when later she reached out to switch off her bedside-lamp. They could be taken two ways—either that he was genuinely concerned for her welfare, or that he meant to check that she was performing her duties as Heather's stepmother to his satisfaction.

She put an arm up under her head on the pillow, her eyes thoughtful as she stared at the darkened ceiling. Tonight the two of them had tacitly declared a truce, yet Glenn was still the same man who had pinioned her with his cold, contemptuous gaze while Stuart was alive. And this evening, even if an uncanny rapport had flickered between them, there had also been plenty of undercurrents and the wayward flaring of an old tension. So how exactly should she class the man who would again inevitably feature prominently in her life now that she was back home? As friend or foe?

CHAPTER THREE

AFTER six months in Provence, the sedate Edwardian house where Kira had lived since her marriage struck her for the first time as sombre. With five bedrooms and three reception-rooms it had been much too large even when Stuart was alive. But she'd been hoping then to have children, and Stuart had liked the chill elegance of the house with its wide drive and leaded windows. For him it had been a status symbol, and it had pleased him the way Kira had furnished the house in keeping with its period. In those early days of their marriage he'd so often made her feel valued.

After his death she hadn't moved, partly because its location in Pinner was so convenient, and partly because she hadn't wanted to introduce any unnecessary change into Heather's life after the shock of losing her father. And perhaps, too, she had been trying to cling to memories, painful though the many reminders were. But now she was home again she was ready at least to consider moving. A small, friendly house would suit her and Heather much better.

There was other evidence of the healing work of time. After Stuart's death she had found a hospital atmosphere stressful, even at St Hero's where the speech therapy unit was well away from casualty. Since her return, although she still reacted differently when she saw the blue flashing lights of the ambulances compared with before the crash, slowly they were once again becoming a routine part of hospital life and not a personal symbol of tragedy.

In fact she was glad to be back at the hospital,

although financially she had no need to work. Stuart had carried a large life assurance, and the death and survivor policy on his part of the business had left her very well off. She had taken Glenn's advice on how best to invest the money in both her and Heather's interests. But, despite the income from it, she couldn't see herself staying at home, not when Heather was growing up so fast. Her work gave her a sense of direction, brought her into contact with new people and made her feel generally that she was coping with the challenges of rebuilding her life as a single woman.

St Hero's occupied a large site where the suburbs petered out into gently rising green-belt land. It was modern with pleasant grounds and, luckily, now that she had given up driving, it was very accessible by public transport.

On Wednesdays the medical team she was part of had its weekly meetings. Getting together with the doctors and the other therapists, both physio and occupational, meant the most effective treatment for rehabilitation patients could be worked out. She was gathering up her notes as the meeting ended when Dr King came over to see her.

He had joined the staff shortly before she had gone on leave of absence and he was obviously pleased she was now back on the team. In his mid-thirties, he was friendly and outgoing. He had light brown hair, a broad-shouldered build and wore steel-framed glasses.

'That was a very useful session we had just now,' he began. 'Are you in a hurry, or could you spare a few minutes? I'll be referring someone to you next week and I'd like to go over the case with you.'

Kira glanced at her watch.

'I'm meeting a friend for lunch,' she said. 'but yes, I've got a few minutes.'

'Good. Let's make it over a quick cup of coffee,' Nigel suggested.

They made their way to the staff-room which was almost empty and sat down at one of the tables. Although she hadn't known him all that long, she found Nigel King easy to talk to. She knew that he was divorced, but he didn't give the impression that he was looking for emotional involvement and she liked their uncomplicated friendship.

They discussed the patient he had mentioned in some detail, and were walking back along the bright length of hospital corridor when he asked, 'Do you happen to be free Thursday week? I've been given two complimentary tickets for the new musical that's just opened in the West End. I was wondering if you'd like to come.'

Surprised by the invitation, Kira hesitated before answering.

'Go on, say yes,' Nigel coaxed. 'It's had very good reviews.'

'OK,' she smiled. 'Thanks. I'd like to come.'

'Great,' he said, touching her on the arm by way of parting as he added, 'Well, I must get started on my ward rounds.'

She met Beth as arranged in the little Italian restaurant not far from the hospital. The two of them had been friends since they'd trained together. Afterwards, when Beth had married and Kira had been working some distance away on the other side of London, they'd kept in touch. Now they lived quite close, Beth's husband, Jon, having moved into his new dental practice locally at about the time Kira and Stuart had got married.

'I hope I'm not late,' Kira began as she slid into the banquette opposite Beth.

'No, I've only just got here myself.' Beth smiled.

As always there seemed a lot to talk about, and the waiter had served them with two generous slices of piping hot pizza when Kira asked, 'How are Rachel and the boys?'

'The twins are a handful,' Beth said good-temperedly. 'But at least school keeps them out of mischief to some extent. By the way, now you're back home, Rachel wants to know, when can Heather come and spend the weekend with us?'

Beth's daughter was almost eight, but despite their age difference the two girls got on well together and every so often stayed the night at each other's houses.

'Heather's been asking me the same question,' Kira said with a smile.

'Then let's keep them both happy and make it this weekend.'

'Fine,' Kira agreed. 'In fact, that would help me. It's the accounting institute dinner on Saturday, so if Heather spends the night with you I won't have to trouble Jean to babysit for me.'

Although the dinner was bound to be marked with sadness, Kira was determined to view it positively. It was some while since she had bought anything new to add to her wardrobe, and she decided to shop for something stylish to boost her morale..

Going into her favourite boutique in Pinner village, she found an irresistible turquoise silk-crêpe dress. Graceful and fluid, it might have been made for her. With its low, draped back it was quite revealing, while hiding the fact that she was scarred from the crash. Worn with sling-backed silver shoes, her bright hair in a french pleat, and the diamond and pearl earrings Stuart had given her, she gave the impression of cool, *soignée* confidence.

She cast a quick glance in the hall mirror on Saturday evening as she went to let Glenn in. The presentation was going to be an ordeal, but it bolstered her courage to know that to look at her no one would guess that behind the façade was an ache of loneliness.

She had seen Glenn only once since their dinner together, which was when he had dropped by one evening to see how she and Heather were. The truce between them had continued.

Kira had always been very independent. Apart from her dislike of Glenn, that was another reason why, once she'd rallied from the first shock of grief, she'd refused to rely on him any more than was absolutely necessary. It was only now they were beginning to forge a bond of friendship that she was prepared to concede that there were certain advantages in not being completely alone with the responsibility of bringing up Heather. Perhaps if this mood of tolerance between them continued they'd be able to make the right decisions for her stepdaughter together.

She opened the front door and was momentarily arrested by his dark good looks. In a dinner-jacket with a black bow-tie, he was swarthy and urbane, every line and plane of him exuding strength and masculinity.

She saw his gaze travel over her and as it did her greeting died away. Glenn's blue eyes had never raked her so blatantly before, seeming to generate heat all through her. Unsettled to a degree she couldn't explain, she snapped, 'Well, what's the verdict? Do I qualify for entry into your harem?'

Her words were met by a silence increasingly filled with a curious static. Unable to drag her gaze away from his, she had time to regret her hastily flung words before he asked leisurely, 'Is that your aim, Kira?'

Her eyes, already turbulent, flashed with anger, even though she'd more than deserved the comment. She'd never heard his voice have a sensual inflection and, not liking the prickle that traced down her spine in response to it, she said coldly, 'I've *no* desire to be the latest addition to your string of women.'

'No, in any string I imagine you'd want to be the centre pearl.'

She wasn't sure how to interpret his remark, and she certainly didn't intend asking him to explain it. Determinedly she brought her temper back in check. Their relationship had improved too much of late for her to want to wreck it for no good cause. In a cool, but pleasant enough voice, she said, 'I'm all ready, so shall we go?'

Something flickered in the depths of his eyes and her heartbeat quickened as though she sensed danger. But he did not comment on her abrupt switch of mood with him. His faintly amused forbearance made her yet more conscious of the firmness of his personality. It was his forcefulness coupled with the strength of his physique that seemed to put her on the defensive.

They left the house and when she didn't call out goodbye Glenn asked. 'Where's Heather tonight?'

'She's at Beth's,' Kira answered, going on to talk about the little girl.

She was still rebuking herself for the senselessly provocative opening comment she'd made to him. She was going to find the evening ahead taxing enough without adding to it a clash with Glenn. Not even their truce seemed able to prevent wayward vibrations developing between them, which led inevitably to her flaring up with him.

The reception area in the mezzanine of the opulent London hotel was already full of people when they arrived, the men's evening suits the perfect foil for the kaleidoscope of colour provided by the women's dresses. It was the first large social function Kira had attended as Stuart's widow, and she felt tense. She wondered if Glenn sensed it, for he promptly took a drink for her from a tray carried by one of the passing waiters and his hand was at her elbow as they were swept into a group of mutual acquaintances.

Sipping the champagne helped her to relax. Glenn saw to it that she circulated and, with so many people that she knew through her husband, she was kept fully occupied smiling and making small talk.

Yet all the time she was aware of a new and strange current of magnetism linking her and Glenn. It was inexplicable and unsettling. She didn't even need to glance at him to be conscious of his height and the mature power of his build. It might be illogical, but she found herself resenting his gentlemanly vigilance towards her. Perhaps it was better when they'd been enemies. She had built a citadel around her emotions since Stuart's death and didn't want anyone prowling about the walls. That was how Jericho had fallen.

They had just turned away from the group they were with when a striking-looking woman paused deliberately to make an entrance at the head of the regal staircase. She was wearing a Spanish-style black lace evening-dress that was every bit an exotic as she was. Its short fandango skirt showed off wickedly long legs in sheer black stockings, while its gold embroidered bodice was slashed in a plunging V.

As heads turned she tossed back her raven hair almost impudently, her pose studied yet nonchalant. The light caught on the heavy jewellery at her throat and wrists and gleamed off her ivory-smooth shoulders.

Though she had arrived alone, a tall blond man, evidently her partner for the evening, immediately went to welcome her. Putting a slim, comradely hand on his arm, she dismissed him temporarily before approaching Glenn.

She reached up to brush his cheek with her lips.

'I shouldn't have let my membership lapse,' she began, her voice an intimate caress. 'Thanks so much for getting me a ticket at the last minute.'

'My pleasure,' Glenn answered with an attractive indulgent smile. 'That's quite a dress you're wearing.'

'I'm glad you like it, Glenn,' she purred.

She succeeded in making his name sound as personal as an endearment, and Kira felt an odd stab, almost akin to jealousy, go through her. Quickly she schooled her expression to one of polite interest as, turning to her, Glenn said, 'Clare's just joined us as an auditor. Clare, I'd like you to meet Kira Newall.'

'I'm sure you'll enjoy working for the firm,' Kira said amiably. 'It's very friendly.'

'So I've found already.' Clare's eyes were as dark as sloes as they met Glenn's in a soft, meaningful glance. 'Though as it happens Glenn and I are friends of long standing. We were at university together.'

'That's going back a bit,' Glenn said with a laugh.

Kira hardly needed confirmation of the bond between them. They had all the easy familiarity of lovers. Doubtless, had he not been obliged to escort her as his partner's widow here this evening, he would have come with this sultry gypsy. She squared her shoulders imperceptibly. Seeing Glenn being as charming as only he knew how with a woman wasn't new to her, but never before had she been ruffled by it.

Perturbed by her reaction, it was only when she heard Glenn speak her name that she realised she had momentarily lost track of the conversation. She came back to it to hear him say, 'It was Kira's husband who founded the firm.'

'How simply awful for you that he was killed like that,' Clare said with a rush of sugary sympathy. 'But you've got a little girl, haven't you? I've always thought that once you've borne a child by a man, nothing can really separate you.'

Kira's fingers tightened on the stem of her glass. Clare had no way of knowing that her remark would hit a nerve, that she was barren. Although in some ways accepting her failure to conceive was less painful than the constant strain of unfulfilled hope had been, a sharp, cruel pang still went through her.

'Heather's my stepdaughter,' she said. 'I was Stuart's second wife.'

She hated being put in the position where she was

having to explain her life to a patronising stranger. The evening was strain enough without having to endure Clare's honeyed insincerity. Catching sight of some friends, she said lightly, 'If you'll excuse me, I must just say hello to June and Andy.'

But although Glenn obviously enjoyed talking to Clare he was too urbane to neglect Kira for long. He rejoined her as the guests began to drift into the ballroom. She had a strong desire to tease him about his gypsyish companion but she checked the temptation, knowing that her teasing would sound barbed. In any case, his love-life was of no interest to her.

They were seated at the long, top table that was reserved for the institute's key officials and their wives. Glenn had acted as the organisation's treasurer for the last two years, a position Stuart had coveted and manoeuvred for. It was strange, she reflected, that the two men had been friends when there had always been, certainly on Stuart's part, a strong sense of rivalry between them. Perhaps it had been inevitable when they'd both been so evenly matched with the same qualities of ambition and determination.

After the coffee had been served the lights were dimmed to focus attention on the microphone in front of the band for the chairman to make his address. As he spoke, Kira found herself thinking back to the last institute dinner she had attended. Then Stuart had been alive . . .

Glenn touched her arm, rousing her from her thoughts. He spoke quietly, 'Your turn now, Kira.'

Steeling herself, she rose and accompanied him to the microphone. The applause for the chairman died down, and in the silence she stepped into the well-focused incandescence of the baby spotlight. She felt nervous and flashed a glance at Glenn, seeing his rapier-sharp eyes almost smile encouragement to her.

It was curious that *he* should be responsible for the

confidence that helped her to begin. She had thought her speech out carefully but she had not memorised it, so her words held both spontaneity and warmth as she paid tribute to the high professional standards her husband had been dedicated to. The recipient of the prize came forward to shake hands with her and immediately the ballroom burst into genuine and affectionate applause, making her eyes smart because she was so touched.

With the speeches made and the toasts drunk, the band struck up its opening dance number. The chairman asked her to partner him and, relieved that the presentation was over, she accompanied him on to the floor to start the dancing.

When she returned to their table it was to find that Clare had joined it. She was sitting with one arm resting against the back of her chair, her body turned slightly so that Glenn could appreciate her long, shapely legs in their cloud of black lace and net. It occurred to Kira that there wasn't much Glenn's latest conquest didn't know about body language. Normally such a thought would have been coupled with a touch of wry humour. Tonight she felt merely angry. With no desire to intrude on the conversation, she turned promptly to her companion on her left.

She didn't know how it was that she sensed the instant they stood up to dance. Breaking her resolve, her eyes finally strayed to them. It was her bad luck that at that moment Glenn should raise his head. The swirl of movement on the dance-floor receded into insignificance as their gaze met, his with a hint of speculative mockery, hers stony and enigmatic.

She was diverted by her neighbour refilling her glass. Too late to refuse more champagne, she drank it in an attempt to conquer her ridiculously turbulent mood. Why on earth should she be letting the sight of Clare moving sinuously with Glenn nettle her like this? She

had always disliked the man so it couldn't possibly be
jealousy. Had she unconsciously become so dependent
on him in the last year that she now resented any
encroachment on their relationship? It might be a wild
thought, but even so it was alarming.

It was some while later when a man's warm hand
grazed her back. She didn't even have to look up to
know whose touch it was.

'Would you like a dance?' Glenn asked.

To an outsider there was no evidence of friction in the
way she turned to him, but Glenn was too astute to
miss the momentary flash of rebellion in her eyes. His
voice held a note of warning as he lowered it to say, 'I
was Stuart's business associate and friend. Try to
remember that, because it will look very strange to
everyone here if we shun each other.'

He only had to issue her with a veiled order for her to
long to defy him. Yet she knew he was right. With well-
feigned surprise she said, 'What a strange thing to say!
I've no intention of shunning you. In fact, I was hoping
you'd ask me to dance.'

She knew the deft hypocrisy of her words wouldn't
be wasted on him. They'd had too long a history of
veiled antagonism and there was too much telepathic
communcation between them. The glint she saw in his
gaze told her he was both vaguely amused and
annoyed by her reply.

They were old hands at dissembling in public, but
this time there was a subtle difference in her coolness
with him. She realised as they danced together she
wanted to needle him. Quite why, she couldn't fathom.
Until tonight her aim had been to consolidate their
truce. But now, sensitive and fiery from the stress of the
presentation, she wanted to get under his skin, and by
being distant and yet gently bewitching she sensed she
was doing just that.

Glenn had made her smart with silent resentment on

so many occasions in the past, it was good to be exacting a little revenge. Certainly it was an antidote to the pain she was feeling. It wasn't until it was time for them to leave that she wondered how wise it was to provoke a man who doubtless could be dangerous.

CHAPTER FOUR

WHILE Kira went to fetch her shawl, Glenn paused to say goodnight to Clare, strolling with her out on to the mezzanine as though they were reluctant to part. The two of them were still together when Kira returned from the cloakroom. Even at a distance she could see that Clare was turning on her full smouldering charm with him.

It seemed he sensed her presence, for, with a slight frown, he immediately glanced across the mezzanine in her direction. She hadn't meant him to see she was watching him. Their gaze clashed before he bent his head to kiss Clare lightly on the cheek. It was the sort of casual goodbye that somehow suggested a deeper intimacy in private.

Hurriedly Kira averted her gaze under the pretence of draping her shawl around her shoulders as Glenn advanced towards her. She didn't know why she should feel so furious with him. Tonight had been difficult for her, and Glenn had been both considerate and supportive, so why was she simply spoiling for a fight with him?

Curbing her temper, she remarked carelessly as he joined her, 'It was good of you to bring me tonight, but I hope I'm not cramping your style.'

'Clare's most understanding, but I'm touched by your concern,' he answered with the merest inflection of irony. 'But if any further explanations are needed I'll sort it out with her tomorrow evening.'

She felt a surge of irrational indignation that he should spell out his relationship with Clare so clearly to her, and sought to bring her emotions under control. It was nothing to her whom Glenn dated or slept with, and whatever the strain of the evening, it was no justification for her sarcastic comments.

The trouble was that after a year of seeking to avoid pain with a kind of inner numbness, the presentation had left her nerves raw. She could no longer rely on her usual stoicism. It seemed to have been stripped from her so that behind the façade of poise she was hurting and ready to over-react.

Slightly ashamed of her contentious behaviour with him, she tried to make amends by being compliant in the car. She might have succeeded if there hadn't been such an atmosphere of tension between them.

They drove home along roads that were quiet and golden with the glow of the street-lamps. The tranquillity of the night seemed to emphasise by contrast the undercurrents between them, and she was thankful when he finally drew up outside her house. A few words of thanks to him for helping her through the evening and she could escape from him without the mood of confrontation coming to a head.

As he pulled on the brake he said, 'Tonight would have been a good opportunity for you to drive. The roads are always empty after midnight. A pity I didn't see to it that you switched to soft drinks after the toasts.'

'Are you saying I've had too much champagne?' she said indignantly.

In the shadows of the car she saw his amused smile. He removed the ignition key, obviously intending to see her safely to the door, and answered, 'I'm saying you've had just enough to be less inhibited with me than usual.'

'I don't know what you mean,' she said coldly, uncomfortable that he obviously knew she had set out to aggravate him.

'Perhaps I was mistaken,' he said with deft sarcasm. 'Perhaps you actually *meant* to play the subtle temptress with me.'

'How *dare* you?' she breathed.

'From your outraged reaction I'll give you the benefit of the doubt and assume you didn't know how provocative you've been,' he said, grazing her cheek lightly with one finger. 'But just the same, don't repeat the performance, not unless you're prepared to take the consequences.'

She shied away from the insolent caress.

'You arrogant . . .'

Instinct warned her not to accelerate the exchange, and she broke off, glaring at him before she got out of the car, anger in every line of her slim body. It infuriated her that she was always in the position of owing him gratitude so that she couldn't speak her mind. Though possibly she wouldn't have dared in any case. Glenn wasn't someone to court trouble with. And in this instance right wasn't entirely on her side. She certainly hadn't meant to do anything other than needle him, but perhaps to a man her cool, subtle charm might have seemed a deliberate enticement.

Putting the key in the lock, she opened the front door. She touched the switch for the hall light and was turning to say a brusque goodnight when there was a flicker and then darkness.

'Damn!' she exclaimed softly. 'The bulb must have blown.'

'It's more than that, I'm afraid,' Glenn said. 'The porch light's gone off, too. A fuse must have blown. Find me a torch and I'll fix it for you.'

'Thanks, but I'll manage.'

For an answer he marshalled her firmly inside and shut the front door behind them.

'What makes you so stubborn?' he asked impatiently.

She pulled away from him. She didn't like the way

that lately her heart seemed to jolt whenever he laid a hand on her.

'I like to be independent,' she said fiercely.

'Well, for once you'll have to sacrifice that. Now, do you have a torch?'

There was a moment's silence, and then, capitulating because she had no other choice, she said, 'Yes, there's one in the kitchen.'

'Then can I suggest you go and fetch it?'

'Will you stop treating me like a five-year-old?' she flared in retaliation to his tone.

Her eyes had adjusted to the gloom by now and she caught the flash of his smile. Since her return from France she seemed to have annoyed and amused him in roughly equal parts. It had surprised her to discover what a quick sense of humour he had. She had always thought him dour, and perhaps had there not been so much tension still between them she might now have appreciated his wit.

Instead she swept away from him across the large reception hall. She knew exactly where the torch was and, despite the darkness, she was soon back with it. Glenn was shrugging off his jacket.

'It goes to show everyone's luck has to change some time,' he said. 'I never thought I'd get you alone in the dark.'

'I don't find that funny,' she snapped.

'You're surely not afraid to share a joke with me, are you, Kira?'

'Not so long as it *is* a joke,' she answered.

He handed her his jacket as he took the torch. The fact that he was a good six foot two and that she had to look up to him so much increased her wary defensiveness.

'Look,' he said drily. 'Let's forget what I said in the car. Obviously you've no idea how provocative you can be.'

She dropped her gaze and he turned, ducking his head as he went into the cupboard. The dimness made her more aware of the warmth his jacket retained from his body and the fineness of the cloth. She caught herself caressing the weave with her fingers and hurriedly hung the jacket on the newel post.

While Stuart had been alive there had never been one spark of awareness or rapport between her and Glenn—not on her part, and she would have said with equal certainty not on his. He'd always made his contempt for her very plain. But tonight there were unmistakable undertones in his remarks that made her angry and uneasy.

She had no wish to form a serious relationship with any man, let alone a transient one with *him*. Her life consisted of Heather and her work at the hospital, and that was the way she intended it to stay. She still missed Stuart too much to believe she could ever fall in love again. That, together with her doubts about her fertility, made her certain that she would remain both single and celibate.

'I've found some fuse-wire,' Glenn called to her. 'Come and hold the torch and I'll have the lights back on in just a minute.'

She followed him into the confined space. In the gloom, and restricted by the various household tools and cleaning equipment, she seemed to be almost on top of him. She took the torch from him, angling the yellow beam of light while he unscrewed the lid from the fuse-box. The wiring of the house was old, and, making the job more difficult, none of the fuses was labelled.

Glenn frowned slightly and said in a preoccupied voice, 'If you intend staying here, you ought to get the house rewired. Lights don't fuse unless there's something wrong. There must be some bare wires touching somewhere and that means a fire risk.'

'I'll get it seen to,' she promised.

She was glad of his prosaic conversation. She was beginning to think the champagne had had some effect on her, after all. If she had a clearer head perhaps she wouldn't be so acutely aware of him. Crouched down on his haunches with the stairboards above them, he seemed too big and too close.

She noted the play of his pristine white shirt across his back as he worked, the gold Omega watch on his swarthy wrist. She fought to repress the memory of how it had felt to dance with him this evening. He hadn't held her closely but then he hadn't needed to. Even without heightened body contact they had moved as one, his body guiding and controlling hers effortlessly. She touched her fingers lightly to her french pleat, nor sure whether it was the enclosed space or a flush of sexual awareness that was making her hot.

'Can you hold the torch a bit higher?' Glenn said, turning unexpectedly.

Reaching upwards to where she stood leaning towards him, he took hold of her arm to steady the wavering beam of light. She caught her breath slightly at his touch and hoped he hadn't noticed.

'I'm afraid I don't make a very good electrician's mate,' she said, meeting the faint, quizzical look in his blue eyes.

'Well, you're not exactly dressed for it,' he teased with his disarming smile. Turning back to the fuse-box, he said, 'Right, let's see if that does the trick.'

He reached for the switch and the light immediately came on.

'Marvellous,' she said with a laugh.

'That ought to make you feel less vulnerable.'

Ducking quickly under the low lintel of the door, she glanced back at him, not sure what he meant. She stumbled a little and Glenn put a supportive hand under her elbow and kept it there as they stepped out of the understairs cupboard into the hall.

For an instant she was again frighteningly conscious of how attractive he was. She noted his dark pupils, the power of his body, and realised that perhaps for the first time she was totally alone with him. The knowledge made the appeal of his potent masculinity all the more threatening and, hunting hurriedly for something to break the mood, she managed a shade breathlessly, 'I'll put a new bulb in the hall.'

'No, leave it till I can look at it in the daylight,' Glenn said. 'It's an old fitting and if you change the bulb the fuse will probably blow again. Manage until Saturday and I'll thread a new wire down for you.'

'I don't like troubling you,' she answered. 'I'll get someone round.'

Glenn drew his brows together, mild annoyance strengthening the incisiveness of his manner.

'I can't believe you're as ungracious about accepting help from everyone else as you are with me.'

'We're had this conversation before,' she said. 'I *don't* like being constantly indebted to you.'

'You're scarcely indebted to me over a light fitting,' he said curtly. 'So what makes you so defensive? Are you afraid I'm going to exact payment?'

Immediately her eyes grew stormy. She was completely alone with him and this wasn't the first time tonight that their conversation had veered dangerously towards the intimate. Acutely on edge with him, she said scathingly, 'What are you specialising in tonight? Innuendoes?'

He laughed without a trace of anything other than good-tempered amusement and came back promptly with, 'And what's your speciality? Tart replies?'

His humour was infectious, dispelling the crackling animosity so that she momentarily forget her wariness and laughed contritely. It was foolish to allow him to make her feel so endangered. Glenn was far too experienced with women ever to get into a situation where he got his face slapped.

'I'm . . . I'm sorry,' she apologised. 'I'm afraid I've been short-tempered all evening.'

'Well, at least making the presentation is behind you now,' he said with an understanding that made any more words on the subject superfluous between them.

It was the closest they'd ever come to sharing a moment of quiet trust and friendship, and she smiled at him and then joked lightly, 'I usually offer the electrician coffee.'

'Thanks,' he answered. 'I'd like a cup.'

He went into the drawing-room while she filled the kettle in the kitchen. She set the cups on a tray, automatically adding the sugar bowl. She knew Glenn's tastes well. He preferred his coffee black but sweet, and he drank his Scotch straight. Right from the start she had noticed each small detail about him as though wanting to size up her secret adversary. Stuart, not realising her motives, had once commented on it.

'It's no wonder you're such a perfect hostess,' he had said, putting an arm round her, 'when you bother to remember what pleases people.' In Glenn's case the comment was ironic. Her eyes became remote as she thought of her husband. In the beginning they'd been so happy together. It was only later that she had begun to feel he didn't love her the way she loved him. Now, as a pang of loneliness hit her, once against she wondered where she had gone wrong.

She sighed and, banishing the memories, joined Glenn in the drawing-room. He had picked up the newspaper she had left lying on the sofa and as she passed him his cup he commented, 'I see you've made a start on the crossword.'

'I wouldn't call it a start, exactly, she said. 'I found it harder than usual and I gave up with it.'

'Do you object to a joint effort?' he asked. 'I know

some crossword addicts don't like anyone muscling in.'

'Not me,' she said, slipping her shoes off and tucking her feet up beside her in the armchair. 'I usually do them alone, but they're more fun together.'

He took out a gold pen from his inside pocket and read out one of the clues. Soon they were both thinking aloud, seeming as though by telepathy to arrive at the correct answer after a lively exchange of ideas. She found she was laughing, and setting her coffee-cup aside she went to join him on the sofa.

She studied the newspaper he was holding against his knee, noting without meaning to the lean length of his thigh. The glow from the standard-lamp was restful, the shadows accentuating the slight gauntness of his cheeks, the strong, determined jaw and hawkish brows. She stole a glance at him, thinking that it wouldn't have surprised her if one of his ancestors had been a corsair. Certainly he had something of the swarthy, fearless look of a pirate. Perhaps that was partly what made his urbane charm so unsettling.

'Unmarried, in fun we delight,' Glenn read out, adding, 'That's not a hard one. But perhaps you have a block on the subject.'

'A block on what subject?' she asked with a puzzled smile, knowing he was giving her a clue. 'No, I haven't!' she exclaimed, suddenly seeing the answer. 'It's "unwed".'

'Right,' he agreed, filling it in.

'Though I don't think I'm the one you should accuse of having a block about marriage,' she teased without thinking. 'After all, you're single too.'

He glanced up and their eyes locked.

'That sounds like an invitation to treat,' he mocked softly.

She felt her heartbeat quicken. A tinge of colour came into her face and she said quickly, remembering his warning, 'I'm not flirting with you, Glenn.'

'You do it all the time,' he said, the dangerous silky note in his voice sending prickles of alarm across her skin.

'That's not true!' she said, stiffening.

Glenn tilted her chin up toward him.

'But when I point it out to you,' he said, his voice hardening, 'you go rigid and defensive on me. What are you afraid of? Not me, surely, not now. Of your own emotions, maybe?'

She saw from the tautening of his cheek muscles that he was as tense as she was and, alarmed by the sudden crackling energy between them, she got swiftly to her feet. She would have found it easier to have frozen him with chilly hauteur if she hadn't slipped her shoes off. Barefooted, even standing she felt vulnerable with him.

'My emotions are perfectly under control,' she said stonily.

'They're too much under control,' he said with quiet purpose as he, too, got to his feet.

Despite the effort it cost her, she managed to hold his gaze and stand her ground.

'I happen to like them that way.'

'Suppose we put it to the test,' he said, pulling her to his chest.

'Let go of me!' she demanded, hitting out at him.

'Not this time,' he said with equal vehemence.

He snatched hold of her wrists, rendering her captive. Pinioned against him, she met the blazing blueness of his gaze and saw his eyes travel to her lips. Her heart was pounding with rapid, heavy beats and a tremor of expectancy went through her. It robbed her voice of strength so that she could only say in a whisper, 'No, Glenn, don't you dare.'

'Somehow I don't think you mean it.'

Her breath of protest was lost as he bent his head, the strong lines of his face blurring as his mouth claimed hers. Immediately some intangible current sent an undreamed-of shock of hungry response through her. Glenn couldn't fail to sense it. Immediately he released her wrists, his arms sliding around her as he engulfed her in his embrace. His mouth was fierce and possessive, and her fingers tangled tightly in his hair as her lips pa﹏d willingly under his.

It was as though he had set a spark to a tinder-box and she was helpless to fight against the soaring flames. Her body was pounding with pagan pleasure, desire heating her blood and flushing her pale skin. She scarcely realised the ardency and completeness of her response until Glenn gave a muffled groan deep in his throat and his hands moved lower, making her fully aware of his taut, aroused body.

She flinched and broke the kiss. Turning her head, she gasped, 'Stop it! That's enough!'

'Not for me it isn't,' Glenn muttered harshly, as, cupping her face with his tanned hands, he found her mouth again.

She meant to fight him, but the instant his lips moved over hers weakness swept through her. Her eyes closed, the insistence of his erotic kiss seeming to shake her to the soul. The betraying weakness spread until she was trembling, and when, finally, his plundering exploration of her mouth stopped and he released her, she felt so dizzy she thought she would faint.

She took a faltering step back, staring at him, her eyes huge in her flushed face.

'Kira . . .' Glenn's voice was low and hoarse, his breathing as altered as her own.

She scarcely heard him. A force-field of sexual magnetism was all round her and she was terrified at her vulnerability. She had always hated Glenn, so why had her body welcomed his so fiercely?

'God you torment me,' he said throatily.

'*Leave me alone!*' she breathed, unable to hide that she was trembling. And then, as he took hold of her arm, she gasped on a note of panic, 'I said, leave me alone!'

'Don't,' he murmured. 'Kira, it's all right.'

His voice was husky, but gentle now. He might have been speaking to something half tamed and frightened.

'It's all right,' he repeated quietly. 'I promise you.'

He stroked her hair as he spoke, and suddenly, against his strength and protectiveness, her resistance crumbled. With a faint sob she turned her cheek against his substantial shoulder, pressing tightly to him while his arms went round her strongly.

It wasn't important that she could make no connection between what was happening now and the brutal coldness with which Glenn had always treated her before. What mattered was this closeness, the warm, vital feeling that she was alive after a year of aching numbness. The clean fragrance of his aftershave and the iron feel of his shoulders beneath her fingertips excited her.

Once his blatant indomitable maleness had antagonised her. Now she was unbearably stimulated by it, her slim body again becoming possessed by a feverish madness. She felt his palms travel caressingly across her naked back. A need burned in her to abandon herself to him in a far greater and more complete way. Raising her head, her eyes met the twin blue flames in his in the timeless instant before he bent to taste her lips.

His mouth teased hers, the light kisses they exchanged making her ache for him to give her more of this slow, tantalising pleasure. She murmured in protest when his lips left hers, and then sighed, tilting her head back, when he found the sensitive pulse at the base of her neck.

'Do you know how you intoxicate me?' he muttered raggedly.

She pushed his shirt back from his shoulders, and when his hand cupped her breast she dug her fingers into his back, his name bursting from her lips as he brushed her taut nipple with his thumb. Her heart was thudding wildly, her response adding heat to the conflagration of their desire. She had the sensation she was falling and dimly realised he had lifted her off her feet and was carrying her upstairs, but by now it was too late to escape from the encircling enchantment.

Only when he had laid her naked on the bed did the coolness of the sheets for an instant break the pulsating magic. Her mind started to rebel against what she was allowing and, as Glenn lowered himself to her, she tried to resist.

'No,' she moaned pleadingly. 'This mustn't happen.'

She started to struggle, but immediately he caught hold of her hands, placing her palms flat on his hair-roughened chest.

'Touch me,' he demanded hoarsely. 'God, Kira, don't tease me now.'

'No, please . . .' she whispered, tears starting to her eyes.

He silenced her faint protest, his mouth claiming hers in a deep, urgent kiss as he pulled the slim arc of her against him. Her breasts were pressed against the hard, sculptured muscles of his chest. One thigh moved between hers, making excitement course through her like a raging torrent.

As he bent across her to brand her waist with his kisses, she turned her head feverishly against the pillow, driven to respond to him with an ardent sexuality she had scarcely known she possessed. Glenn's hands and lips adored and caressed her, tendering pleasure upon pleasure which was returned and added to in her hungry need to explore, taste and feel his hard man's body.

As he touched her intimately she gasped, flinching away involuntarily. Instantly he moved position, his mouth claiming hers with passionate demand, his strongly muscled thigh moving over hers. When his fingers returned again to caress her deeply and sensitively she cried out and moaned, feeling him arouse her to a constricting pitch of pleasure so intense she could scarcely endure it. She began to tremble, her thoughts and body afire with the need to be united with him.

Arching against him, she clung to his shoulders, her faint cry drowned by his groan as he took her with a fierceness as though driven by years and years of deprivation. In the ultimate embrace, with no separation of self or of pleasure, she wrapped her slim legs around him before the unbearable joy gathered to explode with cataclysmic force. Her fingernails raked helplessly along the tense muscles of his back as her body blossomed at his thrusting possession of her. A second later Glenn shuddered, his harsh groan of fulfilment coming while she was tumbling into freedom.

Afterwards she lay too spent even to move, her breathing and heartbeat slowly steadying. She felt Glenn move from her, the shift of his warm weight disturbing the all-pervading sense of harmony. He drew her to him with infinite gentleness, retaining the magic before her dazed mind could rebel against the incomprehensive storm of their lovemaking.

His hands smoothed her tumbled hair, cherishing her as they travelled over her body that throbbed faintly with an echo of response. This gentle afterplay was new to her and it stilled the desire she had felt to weep when he had shifted his weight. His tender caresses wrapped her securely in a silken cocoon of sensual peace and, exhausted by the violence of their passion, she was already half-asleep when he murmured, 'You're beautiful, Kira. Beautiful and responsive and so wonderfully giving.'

The darkness made his voice sound loving and hypnotic. Raising her head, she smiled deep into his eyes before pressing a somnolent kiss to his chest as she laid her cheek back against it. His body was warm and powerful, and in moments she had slipped into a sleep that was as profound as the lovemaking they had shared.

CHAPTER FIVE

KIRA stirred into wakefulness, enveloped by a feeling of luxurious contentment. She lay there an instant, lulled and relaxed, before she realised Glenn was lying asleep beside her, his arm thrown across her naked waist. Dazed, she caught her breath. To awaken in his embrace seemed an intimacy yet greater than his physical possession of her.

Last night their impassioned lovemaking had seemed beautiful, the uninhibited sexuality she had discovered a revelation that had made awareness of all else recede. It was only in the light of morning that she felt a sense of shock that bordered on dismay. Since Stuart's death she had shied away from even the possibility of forming another caring relationship with a man. So how was she now lying beside Glenn?

She twisted abruptly to look at him, her mind a whirlpool of questions. The covers had slipped down and she could see the strong muscles of his swarthy chest. His hair was dark against the pillow and even in sleep his saturnine face held a forcefulness of character.

She had never gone to bed casually with a man in her life. Bewilderment and amazment at her behaviour made her eyes darken. Yet as she stared at him, still shaken and uncomprehending, a sweet impulse made her want to reach out and cradle his cheek with her hand. For a moment her concern about the morality of what she had allowed was stilled.

And then, suddenly, Clare flashed into her thoughts. The stirring of a puzzled tenderness was dashed away in a surge of fury and contempt for herself. She had slept with Glenn knowing that there was no emotional commitment between them, when she had seen for herself the evidence of his close relationship with Clare. Her heart pounding, she shrank away from him, about to slither out of bed.

The movement woke him. With a deep sigh he pulled her closer against his naked body. Nibbling her ear, he murmured with a smile. 'I always thought you'd be incredible in bed.'

Shame scorched her. His words left no room for doubt as to how lightly he had taken their night together.

'Don't touch me,' she said between her teeth as she struck her fist against his shoulder.

'What on earth are you . . .?'

'Don't touch me!' she repeated furiously.

Comprehension came into his face. All trace of drowsy humour fled. His eyes narrowed, glinting ominously. Her struggle stilled as his cynicism froze her.

'So you're regretting last night,' he said scathingly. 'That's something of a surprise, considering how wild and abandoned you were at the time.'

'You seduced me last night,' she said, her voice cramped and unsteady.

'The hell I did!' he exclaimed forcefully. He leaned on one elbow, raising himself above her as he scanned her flushed face that mirrored so clearly her distress. He drew a weary intake of breath and said quietly, 'Just what are you upset about, Kira? It's not a crime for a man and a woman to want to make love.'

'I didn't want you,' she lied.

'No?' he flashed back.

'No!'

A glint of dark malevolence came into his eyes.

'Your memory seems a little faulty,' he said. 'Only a matter of hours ago you were shuddering and arching against me. Or have you forgotten how you called my name and raked your nails down my back when . . .'

Humiliated, she swung her hand up, desperate to stop him. She was too distraught to think why he should seem to want to torment her when last night he had deliberately held himself back in his desire, to shower her with pleasure.

But his reflexes were lightning-fast as ever. He snatched hold of her wrist, pushing her back against the pillows, the weight of his body as it came down on hers reminding her that he knew her as intimately as a man can know a woman. As intimately as tonight he would know Clare, she thought, choking back a muffled cry.

'Get off me,' she whispered furiously, her breathing rasping and laboured as she struggled.

'You wanted sex badly last night,' he reminded her gratingly. 'And you got every bit as much enjoyment out of it as I did. So don't try to slap my face this morning, you little vixen. Or I might be compelled to remind you again of how good we can be.'

A tear traced across her cheek and she turned her head away sharply, hating herself that to add to everything she should show such weakness in front of him. Defiantly she glared back at him, expecting to see satisfaction in his face at the ease with which he was dominating her. Instead a nerve jumped in his cheek and, releasing her abruptly, he said with scalding sarcasm, 'Remorse really has set in, hasn't it?'

She rolled away from him, pressing her cheek against the pillow. She desperately wanted to get up, to leave the disturbing warmth of the bed where they had lain together. But it was more than she could manage to walk naked across the room in front of him to fetch her wrap. Trapped, she sensed his eyes on her. Then the mattress dipped and he stood up. He threw her wrap on to the bed, obviously having no difficulty in working out what she was thinking.

'Get dressed,' he ordered. 'You'll feel better.'

'Not with you watching me,' she answered.

He sat down on the bed, putting a hand on her shoulder. She recoiled as if his touch burned her. Shrinking away, she lashed out, 'I want you to leave. You got what you wanted, didn't you? You knew I was vulnerable last night and that it wouldn't take much to persuade me to sleep with you.'

'Kira . . .'

Under any other circumstances the snap in his voice would have stopped her, but now, angry and ashamed, she swept on, 'Do you think I don't recognise the pattern? A little warmth, a little friendship and the next stop's bed. Yes, there are times when I feel sad and I'd like to feel loved. You're not the first man to have worked that out. After all, I'm a widow and that means I'm available . . .'

Glenn grabbed hold of her with a sudden curbed violence that shocked her out of her tirade. He snatched her up from where she was lying and she made a frantic but useless attempt to cover herself. But he seemed not to notice either her nakedness or her scars. His fingers bit into her soft skin as he said with perilously restrained anger, 'If that's the pattern, then it's time you learned to handle the mornings after a little better. But since you obviously need more practice, get out of here before I do something I'll regret.'

He pulled the covers from her and thrust the wrap into her hands. She shrugged it on, her face flaming. Sashing it with unsteady fingers, she fled from the room.

She went downstairs and into the kitchen. Realising she was trembling, she stopped her fraught pacing and pulled out a chair from the table. She sank down on it, resting her head in her hands, until Glenn's lithe tread in the hall made her look up sharply. Her fingers went apprehensively to tighten the collar of her wrap and she got to her feet. But he did not come into the kitchen. Instead she heard the front door bang and then his car start with a roar of acceleration.

As the morning progressed she kept going over what had happened. How *could* she have slept with Glenn? To her, sex had always been an act which only took place within a cherished relationship. To recollect her hungry response to Glenn swamped her with mortified anger. His words taunted her in memory. 'I always thought you'd be incredible in bed.' He had taken her solely to appease a physical need, and she flinched inwardly as she thought of how willingly she had let him seduce her as though neither Clare, nor the old antagonism between them, mattered.

Beth had asked her to Sunday lunch and she set out in good time. Once she was with her friend and her lively young family, perhaps she'd stop reproaching herself so bitterly. She was a brisk walker and it usually took her about twenty minutes to get to Beth's house on the main road. The walk calmed her a little. In time she supposed she would be able to put what had happened into some kind of perspective. At the moment she desperately wanted to forget it.

She was nearly at Beth's when she saw Heather and Rachel coming along from the opposite direction, with Skipper pulling eagerly at his lead. The girls broke into a run, the dog bounding forward, barking excitedly.

'Hello, you two,' Kira smiled. She bent to pat Skipper who was demanding her attention. 'Hi there, Skip.'

'We've just taken him for a lovely long walk,' Heather told her.

'I'm glad you've come early,' Rachel said, slipping her hand companionably in Kira's. 'Will you look through my science homework with me before lunch? Daddy's helped me with it, but he's not as good at drawing as you are, and I'd like to put in some more pictures.'

'Are you trying to get around me?' Kira teased.

They went into the house. An extension had been added across the back of it, providing a large sitting-room with patio doors overlooking the garden. Outside, the six-year-old twins were kicking a football about with their father.

Beth, hearing the sound of chatter and laughter in the sitting-room, appeared from the kitchen.

'Hi, Kira,' she smiled. 'Come on through into the kitchen and I'll make some coffee.'

'Thanks,' Kira answered, conscious that she was already starting to feel less harrowed.

Beth's house, with the children and the dog, was a real home. It was something she'd missed out on and it appealed to her. Like Stuart, she didn't have any close family, only her father now that her grandmother was dead. With him working as the master of an oil tanker, he'd been away for much of the time during her childhood. Her six-month stay in Provence, where he had retired with his French wife, had been almost their first opportunity to get to know each other. Kira's mother had died when she was five and her grandmother had brought her up. Perhaps her childhood explained partly why she'd so very much wanted a family of her own.

'I thought we'd eat just before one,' Beth said.

'Can I give you a hand?'

'You could help me top and tail some gooseberries while we drink our coffee,' Beth suggested.

The two of them chatted easily as they sat at the kitchen table. Through the window Kira could see Heather playing with Skipper in the garden.

'Heather really loves that dog of yours,' she commented.

'Yes, he's a nice old chap. And he's so good-tempered. The twins are always pulling him about and he never gets snappy.'

'It's because he's so used to them,' Kira said. She watched Heather a moment longer and then announced, 'Glenn's arranging for Heather to visit her grandparents this summer.'

'Good idea. I know there was trouble between them and Stuart, but they sound nice people and I've always felt sorry for them not getting a chance to know their own grandchild.'

'I haven't told her yet. I'm waiting till Glenn's booked the flight.'

'He's very good, isn't he, the way he takes his responsibilities as Heather's guardian so seriously?' Beth remarked.

After what had happened between them, Kira found it hard to find a reply.

'Yes, he's most conscientious,' she managed.

'He'll make some woman a very good husband,' Beth observed.

'Probably,' Kira said curtly.

Beth gave her a probing glance, quick to pick up her tone.

'Are you honestly not at all interested in marrying again?' she asked.

'I don't even want to think about it,' Kira said. She tried to lighten the conversation by adding jokingly, 'Now, don't you start on me too. Jean Thorpe who babysits for me is trying to convince me I ought to remarry.'

'OK,' Beth laughed. 'I'll stop. But I will just say that Glenn won't stay single for ever. He's successful and dynamic, and he has a great deal of charm——'

'And you can add to those qualities conceit and ruthlessness,' Kira cut across her, her voice hard.

'Why that outburst? What's gone wrong between the two of you suddenly? I thought you were friends.'

Out of loyalty to Stuart, not even to Beth had Kira ever confided her strong dislike of his partner. Now it was all too complicated to explain.

'Friends?' she said with a trace of bitter mirth. 'If only . . .'

She broke off and Beth prompted, 'If only what?'

Kira made a vague despairing gesture with her hand. Beth had been a confidante for over ten years, and she didn't have anyone else she could confess to. In a constrained voice she blurted out, 'Last night . . . last night I slept with him.'

Beth studied her for an instant before asking in genuine incomprehension, 'Is that so terrible?'

'*Yes*,' Kira said. 'It is.'

'Why?' Beth asked. 'What's wrong with sleeping with a man you're emotionally involved with?'

'I'm not involved,' Kira denied vehemently. 'I can't see how the hell I let it happen.'

'The truth is you're feeling guilty,' Beth told her.

'Guilty over *what*?'

'Over starting to love again now Stuart's dead.'

'Love?' Kira said in sharp surprise.

'Glenn's a very attractive man,' Beth said calmly. 'And you've been widowed a year. Why shouldn't you have fallen in love with him?'

'The reasons, believe me, would fill a book,' Kira replied. 'Beth, I didn't sleep with Glenn because I love him. I slept with him because . . . because I felt lonely, I suppose.'

'What about him? What were his feelings?'

Kira's eyes grew stormy as she thought of Clare. She shook her head, unable to bring herself to admit that he had taken her out of lust.

'When are you seeing him again?' Beth asked.

'In a fortnight's time. We're taking Heather to the zoo as a treat for her birthday.'

'If you ask me, you ought to see him before that. I

think the two of you need to talk.'

'That's the last thing I need.'

There was a pause, and then Beth asked, 'What would happen if Glenn married someone else and he and his wife decided Heather should live with them? I mean, legally, what would your position be? Could he do that?'

This was a possibility that quite simply had never occurred to Kira. For a moment she felt cold with the picture Beth was painting.

'Glenn *could* insist that Heather lives with them,' she agreed, striving to hold down an ominous fear. 'But he wouldn't. Her home's with me. And anyway, even if he were married, I doubt whether his wife would want to take care of Heather. After all, she'd mean nothing to her.'

'Yes, but if I were Glenn's wife, neither would I want him coming round to see you as he does,' Beth pointed out.

'That's ridiculous!' Kira exclaimed, her voice a shade tight. 'She'd have no reason to be jealous of me. Besides, as far as I know, Glenn has no plans for marriage in the near future. He likes playing the field where women are concerned. He always has.'

She tried to dismiss what Beth had said, but it lingered uneasily in her mind. Was Clare nothing more to him than a bed partner, or was he serious about her? If only Stuart hadn't put her in this impossible trap of a situation. She was entirely in Glenn's power, and their night together had put a new tension in their relationship she didn't dare to speculate on. As for Beth's suggestion that she had fallen in love with him, the idea was too crazy to be entertained. He had used her and now nothing would alter her hatred of him.

Glenn was not her only worry. Apprehensive about Heather's trip to Canada, Kira knew she was looking for reasons to delay mentioning it to her. She trusted

Kathryn's parents to be tactful but, feeling as they must about Stuart, they could so easily alter the little girl's opinion of her father. She supposed she was half hoping that Heather would say she didn't want to go, which was both selfish and over-protective. Knowing that made Kira careful that Heather shouldn't sense her misgivings.

As they were walking home after she had met Heather from school on Thursday, she said, 'You'll be breaking up before too long now.'

'I'm glad,' Heather said emphatically. 'I hate the exams we've got at the moment. What are we going to do this summer?'

'Uncle Glenn and I thought you might like to go to Canada to see Grandma and Grandpa.'

'Really?' Heather squeaked. She rushed on excitedly, 'That would be terrific. But you'll be coming, too, won't you?'

'With my job, I don't think I can,' Kira answered. 'I certainly couldn't come for a whole month, which is how long you've been asked for. But I might be able to join you for the last part and we could fly home together.'

'Does that mean I'll have to fly out on my own?' Heather asked.

'Yes, but the air hostessess will look after you. You'll be fine.'

'Oh, I don't mind flying alone,' Heather announced promptly. 'Some of the girls in my class are boarders and they fly on their own when they join their parents for the holidays.'

Kira squeezed her stepdaughter's hand.

'Sometimes you seem to be growing up so fast,' she smiled.

Heather smiled back and looked pleased.

'Why did we never go to see Grandma and Grandpa when Daddy was alive?' she asked. And then, before

Kira could embark on an explanation, she said seriously, 'Was it because my parents broke up when I was little?'

'Yes,' Kira said. 'Your mother and your father each wanted you to live with them, and it made for a lot of bad feeling. But it's time now that was all forgotten. Your grandparents are very fond of you and I'm sure you'll have the most wonderful holiday with them.'

'When am I going?' Heather demanded. 'As soon as school breaks up?'

'Yes,' Kira laughed. 'The very first week of the holiday.'

She had to concede that Glenn had been right over the trip. Heather was thrilled about it. Kira hadn't expected her to show such an adult understanding about the cause of the rift between Stuart and her mother's family. It looked as if there was no need for her to worry any more that she was going to be unsettled by the visit.

Glad that the little girl was so excited, and with her own doubts eased, Kira was ready to enjoy the evening ahead. Nigel was picking her up at seven o'clock for the theatre. She was looking forward to seeing the musical. Yet annoyingly, she couldn't seem to put Glenn out of her mind. Somehow the fact that she'd slept with him in the interval since Nigel had asked her out was there to confuse her.

She decided on a slim, indigo dress with a gentle gathered skirt that she always felt good in. The colour made her eyes more darkly amber and flattered her bright hair. She was fastening her gold hoop earrings when Heather came into her bedroom.

'You look nice,' the little girl said as she sat down on the bed. 'You smell nice, too. I like that perfume. What is it?'

'It's Blue Grass,' Kira told her.

She picked up the atomiser and sprayed Heather's

wrist lightly with perfume. Heather giggled and bent her nose to her wrist.

'It makes me feel grown up,' she said, before asking, 'What time is Mrs Thorpe coming?'

Kira checked her watch. She could always rely on Jean to be on time. She was a kindly woman in her sixties who did voluntary work at the hospital, and although she lived at some distance she was always ready to help out by looking after Heather.

'Any moment now, I should think,' Kira answered. 'In fact, I'm surprised she's not here already.'

Heather watched her while she put on her lipstick and then asked, 'What's Nigel like?'

'He's very nice,' Kira replied. 'Very friendly and easy to talk to. Anyway, you'll meet him before we go out.'

'Is he your boyfriend?' Heather said.

'Don't you like the idea?' Kira queried, quickly perceptive.

Heather shrugged a little and then said with a thoughtful frown, 'No, it's OK, I suppose.'

The doorbell sounded, interrupting them.

'That'll be Jean,' Kira said, thinking that she and Heather must talk about this later. 'I'll go and let her in.'

She was on her way downstairs when the telephone started ringing.

'It's OK,' Heather called out from Kira's bedroom. 'I'll answer it.'

Kira crossed the hall and opened the front door. It was Nigel.

'Hi,' he began. 'I hope I'm not too early. The drive here from my place didn't take me as long as I expected.'

'No, you're not too early,' Kira smiled. 'Come on in.'

'You're looking very charming,' Nigel commented. 'Do you realise this must be the first time I've seen you in mufti?'

From the top of the stairs Heather called, 'Kira, Mrs

Thorpe's on the phone.'

'Thanks, Heather. I'll take it in the hall,' Kira answered before explaining to Nigel, 'Mrs Thorpe's my babysitter. She must be phoning to say she's been held up.'

She picked up the receiver while Nigel went into the drawing-room.

'Hello, dear,' Jean began apologetically. 'I'm so sorry about calling you like this, but I've got a bad migraine. It came on just a short while ago, otherwise I'd have rung you earlier. I'm afraid it means I can't drive over this evening but if you'd like to drop Heather round here . . .'

'No, I couldn't possibly,' Kira said immediately. 'I know what awful migraines you get.'

'But how will you manage?' Jean asked. 'I hate to let you down. Could another friend pop round, do you think?'

Kira remembered Beth mentioning she had plans for that evening, and it was short notice to ask anyone else. Not wanting Jean to worry, she said, 'I'll work something out. You just take good care of yourself.'

Jean said how sorry she was again before ringing off. As Kira replaced the receiver Heather came half-way downstairs.

'Can't Mrs Thorpe come?' she asked, looking over the banisters.

'No, she's not feeling well.'

'You can still go to the theatre,' Heather said generously. 'I'll be all right on my own.'

There was the sound of someone at the front door.

'No,' Kira said as she went to answer it. 'I don't like the idea of your being alone all evening.'

To her surprise and complete dismay it was Glenn. She had been counting on over a week's grace before having to steel herself to encounter him again. The memory of their night together leapt into prominence.

He was wearing a dark grey suit that seemed to retain
the aura of the sharp, hard business world he was so
much a part of. Against his blue shirt his silk tie showed
both good taste and an interesting touch of
individuality. She saw his unfathomable eyes take her
in with a raking glance that missed nothing.

'Hello, Glenn,' she began stiffly, feeling herself
colour hotly.

It was as much as she could manage, but at that
moment Heather, who'd come skipping down the
stairs, exclaimed happily, 'Hi, Uncle Glenn!'

'Hi there, sugar,' Glenn said with an easy smile.
'How are you?'

'I'm fine.'

'I wanted to talk to you,' he said, his glance returning
to Kira. 'But I get the feeling you're off out somewhere.
If so, it can wait.'

By now she had recovered at least a semblance of
poise. She said, 'I *was* going out, but there's been a
change of plan so you'd better come in.'

'If Uncle Glenn stayed, you and Dr King could still go
to the theatre,' Heather put in. 'Then it wouldn't matter
that Mrs Thorpe can't come over.'

For no reason that she could think of, Kira wished
Heather hadn't mentioned that the evening out was
with a date.

'No, pet,' she said a shade tersely. 'I'm sure Glenn
has other plans for this evening. I really don't expect
that.'

'I don't mind standing in at all for Mrs Thorpe,'
Glenn said. He hadn't seemed to react at all when
Heather had mentioned Nigel's name, but his eyes held
a steely light she knew too well for her own comfort.
'That means I'll be able to have a chat with you when
you get back.'

His comment conveyed more than the warning that
they had things to discuss. It implied that he would be

staying after Nigel had gone. She understood that he meant her to be accountable to him. Stirred to defiance, she said, 'We may be late back.'

'Don't worry. I'll still be here.'

For a hot-headed instant she nearly lost her temper. His bland mockery was infuriating. With an effort she said, matching his politeness as though she'd completely missed the silent message behind their conversation, 'Well, if you're sure you don't mind, it's very generous of you.'

Annoyance flashed into his eyes and she had the brief satisfaction of feeling that she could still hold her own with him. That triumph was short-lived. He gave her a mocking glance.

'You can *thank* me later, Kira,' he said with gentle malice.

It maddened her that when she was a widow of twenty-nine Glenn could make her blush like a virgin. But she couldn't flare into anger with Heather present. Instead she said coldly, 'I'll introduce you to Nigel.'

They went into the drawing-room where Kira introduced the two men. Nigel nodded to Glenn with a certain reserve, quite obviously wondering what part he played in Kira's life. But Glenn handled the meeting with his customary urbanity. Kira wondered acidly if he'd ever been in any situation he wasn't entirely the master of. She herself felt suddenly most acutely ill at ease, caught between Nigel, who had asked her out, and Glenn, who knew her very much more intimately.

She could sense a dismaying hospital briskness coming into her manner in her attempt to appear relaxed.

'Well,' she said brightly, 'I think we'd better be going, Nigel, or we'll be late.'

She hoped Glenn wasn't astute enough to pick up that her sole desire at the moment was to escape from him. When inadvertently her gaze met his, there was no gleam of mockery in his eyes, only a piercing directness that conveyed the impression that when she got back the two of them were going to have plenty to say to each other.

CHAPTER SIX

NIGEL waited till they were in the car before remarking speculatively, 'As Glenn is Heather's guardian, I suppose you see quite a lot of him.'

'He calls round occasionally,' she answered.

'He's not married?' Nigel queried.

'No,' she said almost shortly. It was ridiculous to suppose that the vibrations between her and Glenn betrayed the fact that they'd been lovers. 'Why all the interest?'

Nigel turned his attention briefly from the road to give her an engaging smile.

'Because I'm wondering if I have a rival. Do I?'

She bit back a half-angry denial. If she hadn't slept with Glenn she would have treated his remark with playful flippancy. As it was, she felt thoroughly unsettled, conscious suddenly that her ties to Glenn were somehow more complicated than she had supposed. It was not a thought she wanted to explore. With an effort she teased, 'If you're not careful, Nigel, I'll start to think you're getting serious about me.'

'Would that be such a bad thing?' he asked, matching her tone.

'Yes,' she joked back, 'because we're seeing a musical comedy, and if we get intense now, it'll just ruin it.'

Nigel laughed and Kira smiled at him, determined to relax.

With the hospital and their work in common they found plenty to talk about as they drove up to the West End. Nigel was a comfortable person to be with. She wanted to remain unattached, but if she were ever to change her mind it would be this type of sane, secure friendship she would look for, not a blind, reckless passion.

The musical was both spirited and amusing, and soon Nigel was totally absorbed in it. He'd brought a box of chocolates. It rested on Kira's lap and occasionally he almost absent-mindedly took a sweet. There was something boyish about his deep, chuckling laughter, something rather endearing. Kira glanced at him in the red-plush darkness of the dress circle and found herself smiling.

Turning her attention back to the play, she was conscious of a sense of defiant independence from Glenn. She had given her heart when she had married Stuart and she knew what it was to find love increasingly answered by indifference. So never, never would she be fool enough to become emotionally entangled with a man who had always despised her.

Diverted from her thoughts by the witty dialogue on stage, when the curtain finally fell on the last act she joined in the noisy applause with real appreciation. Nigel leant towards her to say, 'I haven't laughed so much for ages. Being given those tickets was a bit of luck.'

'It was. I really enjoyed it.'

'There's no chance, I suppose, of persuading you to have a quick drink somewhere before I take you home?' Nigel said, as taking her hand they followed the crush out of the auditorium.

'It will make us too late getting back,' she said. 'Come in for coffee instead.'

She would have asked him in anyway, but just the same she was aware that there was a measure of rebelliousness against Glenn in her invitation. Whatever he assumed, not in any way was she going to be accountable to him, and she intended establishing that quite clearly.

They got back just after eleven. Heather had gone to bed and Glenn was watching a documentary about property deals in the city. Comfortable in one of the armchairs, his long legs stretched out in front of him, he looked as though he had settled in.

'I wasn't expecting you for a while yet,' he remarked negligently as he stood up and lowered the volume on the television.

'Kira didn't want to encroach on your time too much,' Nigel said, rather pointedly.

Kira felt her heart sink at his tactlessness.

'You shouldn't have hurried, Kira,' Glenn said lazily. 'I told you when I said we had things to talk about, I'm in no rush tonight.'

His voice might be casual, but a keenness that Kira recognised had come into his eyes. It was the keenness of a man made suddenly intolerant of what hitherto had been an annoyance he was prepared to overlook.

She said evenly, 'I'm making coffee. Would you like a cup?'

'I'll make it,' he offered. 'I expect you'd rather chat to Nigel.'

What she'd have liked would have been to have slapped him. It certainly wasn't the first time he'd made coffee in her house. In the years since she'd been widowed he'd looked in often and was quite at home in her kitchen, but his offer very much made it seem as if Nigel was the only visitor. She knew he had done it calculatedly and she was angry, knowing that he intended to make Nigel leave. In every situation he always seemed to win.

Nigel, obviously made uncomfortable by a set-up he couldn't quite grasp, finished his coffee and then stood up to go. Kira saw him out. In the hall he paused, as though wanting to ask her about Glenn but not liking to.

'Well,' he said with determined cheerfulness, 'it's

been a nice evening. Thanks for coming.'

'It was a lovely evening,' she agreed, all the more warmly because the last half-hour seemed to have killed it completely.

'Goodnight, then,' he said, before to her surprise he suddenly bent and kissed her.

It was just a friendly, token goodnight kiss, but somehow Kira felt jumpy about accepting it with Glenn in the drawing-room.

Returning to him after Nigel had driven away, she walked briskly over to the sofa, steeling herself to say with cold, business-like conciseness, 'Well, you've got me alone,' which is what you wanted. So what do you want to speak to me about?'

He was standing by the long sweep of curtains at the french windows. She'd left the collection of American short stories she was reading on the piano, and he'd picked it up to glance at the blurb on the back cover. His fingers on the book's spine were agile and tapering as he set it back and fixed her with a penetrating glance.

'How long has this been going on?' he asked with ominous quiet, a perceptible edge of derision to his voice.

'I take it you're talking about Nigel,' she said chillingly.

'What else?' he replied.

'Then it's end of discussion' she told him, staring back at him.

She kept her gaze level and cold, misled into thinking she could, if she was determined, return their relationship to its former remoteness. Saturday night had been some kind of wild aberration, and the slow, burning anger she now sensed in Glenn pleased her. It made her feel more sure of herself, more certain that, though he'd made love to her, emotionally she was still as inviolate as if he'd never touched her.

'There's no need for you to stand there like a statue

carved of ice,' he said tauntingly. 'Sit down and we'll start again.'

She disobeyed him until he took a step towards her. Feeling threatened, she dropped into the nearest armchair, saying with a surge of antagonism, 'Don't play inquisitor with me, Glenn. I don't owe you any explanations about Nigel. He's a genuinely nice person with a lot of good qualities you couldn't possibly appreciate.'

'Such as warmth and friendliness,' Glenn supplied, the hardness of his eyes curiously at variance with his soft mocking tone.

'Yes, both of those,' she agreed.

'Then it's just as well he didn't stay.'

'And what exactly is that supposed to mean?' she asked coldly.

'A little warmth, a little friendliness, and the next stop's bed.' Glenn quoted her comment back to her.

She sprang to her feet, her eyes dark with anger, her pretence of calm iciness shattered.

'You keep your vile asumptions to yourself! Despite what you obviously believe, I don't sleep with every man who makes a pass at me! You're the only . . .'

She checked herself and broke off abruptly.

'Now that's an intriguing comment you were about to make,' he said quietly. 'Why don't you finish it?'

But she had recovered from the first blaze of anger and she was not to be tripped up again. She was never going to tell him he was the one man she had ever slept with apart from her husband.

'You're the only one who thinks I'm cheap,' she ground back. 'Nigel, on the other hand, respects me and he's far too much of a gentleman for the thought of getting me into bed to have even so much as crossed his mind.'

'However noble his sentiments,' Glenn said sarcastically, 'I'd be very surprised if he hasn't at least imagined what you'd be like to sleep with.'

The fact that Glenn didn't have to imagine made her blush hotly.

'Not all men view women as nothing more than prospective bed partners the way you do,' she flashed back.

'Oh, I'm sure Nigel sees you as a lot more than that,' Glenn said, his words swift and sarcastic. 'Undoubtedly he sees you, too, as a rich widow with a house worth close on three hundred thousand pounds, before we even consider your other investments.'

'You really are despicable!' she exploded. 'Or have you also been adding up my assets?'

'I'm an accountant. Of course I know what you're worth,' Glenn answered, ignoring her temper. 'And it's more than some charmer on the hunt for a rich wife.'

'Nigel's not like that,' she snapped. 'He's never once mentioned money in all the time I've known him.'

'And how long is that?'

Stubbornly, she refused to answer.

'I said, how long have you been seeing him?' he repeated.

'That is none of your damned business,' she flared.

'Whether it is or not, you'll answer me,' Glenn said, catching hold of her wrist.

'I work with him, but tonight was our first date,' she said, adding when still he didn't release his cruel grip, 'I've known him about a year. Now let go of me.'

He released her and, bitterly resentful of his interrogation, she stepped back, rubbing her wrist that showed red marks from the force of his fingers.

'Well, he's certainly taking it nice and slowly, isn't he?' Glenn remarked, the old suave mockery that had been briefly lost in his relentless questioning of her back in his voice.

'And what's wrong with that?' she asked, vaguely

aware that the flashpoint of confrontation was finally over, toned down to a muted hostility.

'Nothing,' Glenn said, sitting down. 'Except that you seemed to resent being seen as available the other night.' She looked away sharply and he reminded her. 'Your term, Kira, not mine. So don't let Nigel take you for an easy target. You're a very rich widow and you're a naïve fool if you don't realise there are a lot of sharks about.'

'And I suppose it's never crossed your mind that Nigel might actually like me simply for what I am?'

'No, I don't discount it,' Glenn said evenly. 'Maybe I'm maligning him, but I'm not usually wrong about people.'

'How nice for you,' she said with petty spite.

She was instantly ashamed of her sharp tongue. Further, she wondered just how much blatant antagonism Glenn would tolerate from her. There was a short silence and then he asked, 'So, are we going to work this out, or are we going to go on behaving as if Saturday night never took place?'

'Because you're Heather's guardian,' she told him. 'I have no choice but to be polite to you. If not, you'd know exactly what I think of you and you wouldn't be tolerated in this house for one minute.'

There was a pause and then Glenn replied, a perceptible note of restraint in his voice. 'I take it you're still holding me entirely responsible for the fact that we slept together.'

'If you don't mind, I'd rather not talk about it,' she said tightly, as she walked to the drinks cabinet. But before she could select a bottle his hands came down on her shoulders, turning her to face him.

'Well, that's just too bad, because like it or not, we're going to talk.'

'Then all right, yes, I *do* blame you for what happened,' she flared. 'You've always struck me as a

man who gets exactly what he wants, so why shouldn't
I hold you responsible?'

'Because you're a woman, and adults usually take
responsibility for their own actions,' he erupted with a
sudden loss of patience. 'My God, what's wrong with
you? Why all this angst because you're attracted to me?'

'Attracted to you?' she repeated, her eyes blazing. 'I
loathe you. But now we are talking about what
happened, let me make it very clear—the fact that
you're Heather's guardian does not give you *droit du
seigneur* over me!'

She saw his jaw tighten. She gasped as for an minute
she thought he was going to shake her, but completely
unexpectedly he then let her go, bringing his anger
swiftly in check. She looked up at him, pale and uncomprehending, and then heard Heather's light tread
in the hall. Quickly she moved away from him in the
instant before the little girl came into the room.

Heather was barefooted and in her nightgown. Her
hair was tousled and her eyes miserable and a shade
muddled from sleep. Kira went towards her, avoiding
Glenn's gaze.

'What's wrong, honey?' she asked, surprised that her
voice could sound so normal when less than a moment
ago there had been such agitation and electricity in the
air. 'Have you had a nightmare?'

Heather shook her head and came close for a reassuring cuddle.

'I've got tummy ache,' she said in a small voice. It
woke me up.'

Kira brushed her hand under the little girl's fringe.

'You don't seem to be running a temperature,' she
said. 'But you shouldn't be wandering about in bare
feet.'

'Pop back to bed,' Glenn told her kindly. 'Get snug
under the covers and Kira will come up and see you in a
minute.

'You won't be long?' Heather pleaded, looking up at her with anxious brown eyes.

Kira gave Glenn a cool glance. Her voice was affectionate, though she meant him to take note of her remark.

'Not a moment longer than I have to be.'

'OK,' Heather agreed. ''Night, Uncle Glenn.'

'Goodnight, sweetheart.'

Kira waited till the little girl had gone out, and then said derisively, 'You weren't exactly going for gold with avuncular sympathy, were you, sending her straight back to bed?'

She was in no mood to care that her comment was unjust. With Heather, Glenn was invariably both kind and patient. All that mattered was defending herself by attacking him with whatever means were to hand.

'There's no sense in her getting cold down here,' he answered, his voice clipped.

'Or were you thinking we still had things to discuss?' she said, her tone coldly scathing.

'That would be rather a waste of my time, wouldn't it?' he replied sarcastically. 'Discussing things, it turns out, isn't one of your strong points.'

'Where you're concerned, I doubt that I have *any* strong points.'

'There are one or two that come to mind.'

She drew a quick, angry breath. His meaning was as stark as if he'd spelled out the insulting implication. In a low voice, fierce with loathing, she said, 'I'd like to forget what happened the other night, and if you were a gentleman you'd let me!'

She would have loved the satisfaction of hitting him, but didn't dare. Glenn's temper had a long fuse, but she knew instinctively it had burned close to the end. Somehow the fact that he had made love to her made even the anger beween them charged now with unpredictable sensuality. She had the vague comprehension that slapping him could quickly lead to sexual grappling.

She went on coldly, 'So *if* there's nothing you want to say to me, I'd like to tuck Heather up.'

'You and I have plenty more to say to each other,' he answered, 'but as now isn't the time, I'll leave you with this.'

He took a letter out of his inside jacket pocket and handed it to her.

'What is it?' she asked with hostility.

'It's from Heather's school, about the open evening. I thought you'd possibly want to come along.'

'Yes . . . yes, I should,' she answered, for once not thanking him for fear that it would choke her.

'Then I'll be going,' he said, tipping her chin up to face him, before mocking softly as he saw the turbulence in her eyes, 'Expecting me to kiss you goodnight, or disappointed that I'm not going to?'

'I ought to slap your face for that!'

'I shouldn't,' he said gently.

She took a wary step back from him. The annoyance that emphasised the attractive, saturnine lines of his face faded and he gave a short, exasperated laugh.

'It's little wonder I find it hard to work you out. I don't think you even know yourself what a hot-blooded woman there is behind that controlled exterior.'

She glared at him, her eyes dark, as she refused to rise to his goading. As though to provoke her further, he grazed her cheek lightly with a caressing finger.

'Goodnight, Kira.'

Again she resisted the impulse to hit out at him and his eyes mocked her restraint, as though he knew exactly what it cost her. Seething, she waited till she heard him leave before she went upstairs to Heather, regretting that she hadn't given way to impulse and thrown something at him.

CHAPTER SEVEN

BY THE following Saturday her temper had cooled enough to mean that she could behave towards Glenn at least with outward composure when they took Heather out on her birthday. It stung her to admit it, but she now realised she couldn't hold him wholly reponsible for the fact that they'd slept together. She could have said no, but she hadn't. Precisely why she hadn't wasn't something she wanted to dwell on.

Heather was fascinated by the zoo, which was always her favourite place for an outing. They had a good look round and then had a leisurely lunch before heading in the direction of the aquarium.

The dimness, after the bright sunshine, together with the shimmering tanks that lined the walls, made Kira uncomfortably conscious of being alone in Glenn's company. Heather had gone on ahead. Hands in the pockets of her dungarees, she was watching some salt-water fish. In the shadowy gloom Kira hunted for an innocuous remark in an attempt to conceal how ill at ease she felt. Instead it was Glenn who broke the silence by mocking softly, 'Relax, Kira. I'm not about to turn the conversation to anything you can't handle. I've already realised you need time to sort yourself out.'

'I don't need to sort myself out over anything,' she replied in a hostile undertone.

'That's not the impression I get.'

'And doubtless you'd know, wouldn't you?' she said scathingly. 'With your vast experience of women, I suppose you can read me like a book!'

He grabbed hold of her arm, swinging her round to

91

face him.

'Exactly where did you get the idea from, that I'm a womaniser?' he asked in a suppressed tone.

'Let go of me,' she demanded.

'I want an answer.'

Other men raised their voices to enforce obedience. Glenn merely had to lower his. As she took a step back, she replied stormily, 'Just how naïve do you think I am? You've had a string of mistresses ever since I've known you, the latest being Clare.'

In the dimness she saw his jaw tighten. In a brusque tone she had never heard him use before, he said, 'Clare happens to be someone special, so I'll thank you not to jump to conclusions about her.'

She didn't know why his words should cause her heart to jolt and then quicken with an almost queasy despair.

'Special?' she heard herself ask huskily. She fought against the constriction in her throat, not knowing how she managed to sound so falsely impassive as she added, 'Are . . . are you thinking of marrying her?'

'Why, are you afraid it might upset our cosy little relationship?'

His sarcasm on top of the turbulence of shock and pain made her erupt into fury.

'I don't give a damn . . .' she began, her eyes blazing.

His hand on her arm warned her and she broke off sharply seeing that Heather was running happily towards them.

'I've been looking at the eels,' she began excitedly. 'Some of them are really huge, Come and see.'

'Perhaps they're conger eels,' Glenn said with a smile as he went ahead with the little girl, giving Kira a few minutes of much-needed space to calm down.

She watched him for a moment, knowing exactly his purposeful walk and the strong line of his shoulders as he listened to Heather's animated chatter. Then abruptly she turned away under the pretence of gazing at one of the softly illuminated tanks. A stingray swam towards the glass and then altered course to float effortlessly away again. She scarcely saw it.

That he should marry Clare was unthinkable! She was so shaken that it took her a minute to recall that he had not given her a proper answer to her question. Thwarted and angry, she had too much pride to ask him again. If she did, he was conceited enough to assume it was because she was interested in him herself! She squared her shoulders imperceptibly as she forced her riotous emotions back in check. Heels tapping smartly on the concrete, she walked to join him and Heather, determined not to give him the satisfaction of seeing how deeply he had jolted her.

It was over the next few days, with time to consider fully what it would mean to both her and Heather if he married Clare, that her uncertainty grew to such agonising proportions. Clare didn't strike her as the maternal type, but she *did* give the impression of being very possessive. Beth's word came back to her. 'If I was Glenn's wife, I wouldn't want him coming to see you all the time.' Doubless Clare would feel the same way. Quite possibly she would insist that Heather go to live with them, and just the wrench alone would make the little girl desperately unhappy.

She only had to think of the brusqueness with which Glenn had told her that Clare was special to him to feel chilly with dismay. She knew that his housekeeper had now retired, and she knew he had made no attempt to replace her. Could that be because he intended marrying Clare? And yet some instinct stronger than reason told her that he *couldn't* be marrying Clare. It wasn't possible when an elusive rapport, that she acknowledged for the first time, existed so strongly between them. She couldn't begin to explain or define it, but neither could she believe that Glenn was unaware of it.

If only she hadn't been so defiant when he'd wanted them to discuss their relationship in the light of the fact that they'd slept together. Maybe then she'd have discovered what his feelings for her were, and she'd know how central Clare was to his life. But now, thoroughly apprehensive, she knew she wouldn't be so obstinate again. Whatever the cost to her pride, she was going to find out where she stood with him.

He called round at seven o'clock on the evening they were to go to Heather's school. Beth had offered to mind the little girl, and they were going to drop her off on the way.

Kira let him in, her manner cool because she felt so nervous. He was wearing a grey business suit. He always looked formidable in city clothes, his attractiveness with an edge of hard urbanity.

'You're a little earlier than I expected,' she began, far more distantly than she'd intended. 'It won't take me a minute to finish getting ready.'

'Before you do,' he said. 'There's something I want to say to you.'

She froze with a sense of dread, her eyes locking with his. She was too late. He was going to tell her he was engaged. Her heart thudding raggedly, she asked, steeled for the worst, 'What about?'

A sardonic gleam came into his blue eyes.

'If I didn't know you better,' he jeered sarcastically, 'I'd almost believe the frigid act you put on for me is for real.'

'God, there are times when I despise you!' she erupted.

'Save it, Kira, and listen to me,' he said. 'Our relationship's deteriorated of late. Tonight, however, we're going to put that to one side. I know what Heather means to you, and how concerned you are for her welfare. I'm sure you realise that this open evening's not going to be much use to anyone if you and I can't even be civil to one another. So just for once, on a subject where we're both agreed, we're going to present a united front. Understand?'

'Was . . . was that what you wanted to say to me?' The ironic quirk of his brow gave his answer in the affirmative and she went on, the tenseness gone from her voice, 'Well, what you've said makes sense to me. In fact . . .' She hesitated and then added in a rush, 'Glenn, I'm sorry if I've been contentious of late. I . . . I haven't meant to be.'

Her apology seemed to clear the air. But she was still, at some point in the course of the evening, going to have to work up to talking about their relationship and what it meant to each of them.

They dropped Heather off at Beth's, stopping only to see her safely inside. Glenn had left a cassette lying on the dashboard and as he restarted the car Kira picked it up.

'Rachmaninov,' she commented. 'Do you mind if I put it on?'

'No, go right ahead.'

The conversation stayed on their shared interest in classical music, and Kira might have been able to relax had she not been aware that Glenn, ever sharply perceptive, seemed to be analysing her every word and gesture. He had always seemed to keep her under close scrutiny. In the past she had interpreted it as silent criticism. Now she wasn't sure what to make of it.

They arrived at the school, where they turned in through the wide gates. Stuart had taken a keen interest in his daughter's education, and the school where she had started at seven was expensive and had a very good reputation academically. Despite the fact that Heather was so young, he'd had definite and ambitious plans for her to qualify, as he had done, as a chartered accountant.

Another car was immedaitely ahead of them, and the Mercedes' engine sank to a purring growl as Glenn followed it at low speed up the drive. A steady stream of parents' cars was arriving, and the main building and outlying blocks had an almost day-time atmosphere of activity about them.

'It looks as if we may have a job to park,' Kira observed. 'The parking area isn't very large and we seem to have hit a busy time.'

'If so, we'll try one of the side roads and walk back,' Glenn answered. 'We've got ten minutes before our first appointment.'

The driver of the car ahead slowed to take a gap immediately in front of the main building and then rejected it as it too awkward an angle and moved on. Glenn drew up just beyond the space, putting the lock on hard on the wheel as, with a bit of very competent manoeuvring, he reversed the Mercedes into it. For an instant Kira forgot the undertone of tension between them and teased, 'That was very neatly done.'

'If you're cheeky, I'll get you to do the driving on the way home,' Glenn answered with an amused smile.

'In which case, I take it back.'

She'd meant to sound flippant, but her voice held a slight note of strain. Starting to drive again wasn't something she could joke about with anyone. She felt the probe of Glenn's eyes, but he didn't comment on her remark. Instead he said, 'If you're ready, let's go on in.'

He put his hand briefly against her back as they walked in through the main entrance. His touch was casual enough, yet even so it sent a flicker of electricity along her nerves. Once he wouldn't have touched her in such a relaxed way. Suddenly she had the panicky feeling that perhaps Glenn meant far more to her than she was prepared to admit. Half angrily she banished the thought. She might not be able to assert her independence from him, but on one point she was adamant. She was never going to love again the way she'd loved Stuart.

Glenn had an adamantine quality to his personality as well as a touch of charm, and Kira was aware that the two of them came across as quite a dynamic couple at the school. She was also aware that it was a perfect possibility that it would be Clare and not her who attended the next open day.

The meetings with the staff went well until they came to Heather's class teacher, Mrs Turner, who conveyed tactfully that Heather was too quiet, reluctant to face a challenge, and seemed to feel unduly pressurised at home. Glenn smoothed the atmosphere of polite dissent and with a flicker of annoyance Kira realised that Mrs Turner had him classed as a reasonable and diplomatic ally against a touchy stepmother.

Her pace was brisker than usual as, the interview over, she preceded Glenn into the corridor.

'Well, you certainly came the lioness in defence of her cub,' he remarked with a trace of masculine humour. 'It was most touching.'

Already on edge, she was in no mood to appreciate his sense of humour.

'Oh, I see,' she snapped. 'You just expected me to sit there and passively agree with what Mrs Turner said!'

Both his eyes and his voice hardened as he said bluntly, 'I didn't expect you to be so over-protective that you'd refuse to hear the truth.'

'The truth?' she repeated with a mixture of hurt and indignation. 'Are you telling me you agree with what Mrs Turner said? Well, for your information, Heather isn't pushed at home. Nor does she have a confidence level of zero!'

'You're exaggerating what was said.'

'Am I?'

'Yes,' he said with quiet ferocity. 'But since you're in the mood for once for frank talking, let's go somewhere

where we can finish this.'

He drove them to one of the popular local pubs. With its low ceiling and dark beams hung with horse brasses, it had a friendly ambience. Glenn ordered their drinks and then steered her to a secluded table in an alcove.

Meaning to forestall the criticism she expected, she said when they'd sat down, 'I suppose it was spending six months in Provence that explains why Heather has done so badly in her exams.'

'I don't think that has anything to do with it,' he answered. 'But just the same, I wasn't altogether surprised by what Mrs Turner told us tonight.'

'So you think I push Heather!'

'I'm talking about the effect that losing her father has had on her,' he said with rapidly eroding patience. 'Plus the fact that for a time after the accident it looked as if you weren't going to make it either.'

'Heather's adjusted to Stuart's death,' Kira said quietly.

'How can she, when you're so cocooned in the past you won't let her forget it?'

She was so stunned by his cruel accusation that it took her an instant to rally.

'Well, thank you very much,' she managed. 'I seem to have cornered the blame from all sides this evening.'

'Don't be ridiculous,' Glenn ordered. 'Heather's extremely lucky she's got you as a stepmother, but Stuart was as ambitious as hell for her, and you've glorified his memory so much that I should think Heather sees achieving whatever he had planned for her as some kind of sacrosanct edict.'

'Then what would *you* suggest, since you have all the answers? I suppose you've decided the school isn't right for her and that she's to go somewhere else.'

'No,' he said. 'This was the school Stuart wanted for her, and she's been fine at it up to this last year. So for now, I'll be satisfied with helping her with her maths in the holidays and booking up driving lessons for you.'

'Driving lessons for me? What are you talking about? I can't see what my driving has got to do with it. And in any case,' she reminded him tartly, 'I've *passed* the test.'

'OK, then, you can drive home.'

She didn't immediately realise that behind the remark was a deadly seriousness of purpose. She retaliated stormily, 'I can't possibly drive home, not when I haven't driven for a whole year.'

'Of course you can.'

His mild reply unnerved her. He meant exactly what he said.

'I thought you were joking earlier when you mentioned it,' she flared, frightened by his quiet firmness. 'But if you weren't, I'm walking home.'

'In those shoes?' Glenn mocked.

'Damn you, I will not be bullied!'

'Did Stuart let you have all your own way?'

'You can leave Stuart out of it,' she said.

'Yes, why don't we?' he agreed. 'It would make life a whole lot easier.'

She was conscious that she was starting to feel hollow and that her hands were trembling. Not wanting him to see them, she slid them deep into her jacket pockets and said with false, cold indifference, '*Are* you driving me home, or am I phoning for a taxi?'

'I thought you cared about Heather a bit more than this,' he said scathingly.

Stung by his contempt, she flashed back, 'I *do* care about Heather, but we're not talking about her now.'

'That's exactly what we're talking about,' Glenn contradicted her, a snap in his voice. 'Every time you go on a bus with her, or accept a lift from a friend, you're reminding her that her father was killed in a car crash. Small wonder she's not over the shock of the accident yet. If you carry on this way, she never will be.'

Kira swallowed and bit her lower lip.

'That's the most *hateful* thing to say,' she said in a husky undertone.

'It's the truth,' Glenn said, apparently unmoved by her emotion. He put his car keys down on the table as he told her, 'If you really care about Heather you'll start driving again.'

For an instant she glared at him. Then she snatched up the keys.

'You always win, don't you?' she said with vehement hostility as she stood up.

They crossed the car park in silence. Kira was fighting a sharp uprise of cold apprehension. She got into the driving seat of the Mercedes which, to accommodate Glenn's height, was placed too far back for her.

'You need to shunt forward a bit,' Glenn told her as he helped her adjust the seat. 'Is that better for you?'

'Yes.'

The curt, monosyllabic reply was as much as she could manage. She was gripped by an almost paralysing sense of alarm that made her want to turn to him, to admit that she lacked the grit to drive again. It was his hard implacability and what he had said about Heather that nerved her against it. He was forcing her to face a monumental fear and she hated him bitterly for it.

Would she never stop blaming herself for the accident that had killed Stuart? Why had she had to insist on driving that day? Stemming the recriminations, she started the engine and switched on the powerful headlamps.

'Relax,' Glenn said with quiet authority, a gentle note of teasing coming into his voice as he added, 'If I wasn't convinced that you're perfectly safe at the wheel, I wouldn't be letting you loose with my car.'

'You just don't understand,' she said, flashing him a resentful glance before she edged the Mercedes forward out of the parking space.

'Put what happened behind you, Kira,' he ordered. 'You could drive for the next forty years and never be involved in another accident.'

She didn't answer. She was too cramped with nerves. She crawled towards the car park exit at almost a snail's pace, but Glenn didn't comment. Similarly, when she waited much longer than was necessary to turn right on to the main road, he didn't tell her it was safe to pull out. She would have liked the reassurance of having instructions. Glenn was making her rely on her own judgement.

Her shoulders felt stiff with tension. Her whole concentration was focused on driving the unfamiliar car. It wasn't until she had negotiated quite automatically the roundabout ahead that she was conscious of a sudden sense of achievement. Until the crash she had enjoyed driving. Gradually she picked up speed till she was doing a steady thirty. She wasn't at ease at the wheel and it would probably be a very long time before she could be, but the first trauma of driving again was over.

Glenn didn't distract her by talking. He switched the car radio on to cover the silence. As she pulled up outside Beth's house, she switched off with an obvious shaky breath of relief.

'OK?' Glenn asked gently.

'Yes,' she answered, and then, because it had to be said, she added. 'I couldn't have done that without you.'

His gaze softened. He cupped her chin with his hand, running the ball of his thumb lightly over her lips, before bending to kiss her fleetingly.

'Maybe a bit of bullying's good for you occasionally,' he said softly, humour in his voice.

She swiftly lowered her gaze before he could see how dazed and helpless his tenderness rendered her. With her heart beating wildly, she said in a rather muffled voice, 'I'll get Heather.'

'No,' he answered. 'I'll get her. You stay where you are.'

'But I . . . I've done my bit of driving for tonight. No, Glenn, please. You take over now. I've had enough.'

'There's no point in half measures.'

'You're pushing me too hard,' she said stormily, certain she couldn't steel herself again after the release of assuming the test to her courage was over.

'It's what you need, but I'm proud of you just the same,' he said, giving her hand a squeeze as he got out of the car.

She stayed staring ahead through the windscreen, ashamed of the way that for no reason her eyes had filled with tears. She blinked them away, thankful that he wouldn't see them and fighting a strange little ache beneath her ribs.

By the time Glenn came down the drive with Heather she was recovered enough to return Beth's cheery wave from the front door. The little girl clambered into the back and then asked in surprise, 'Why are you driving Uncle Glenn's car?'

'Kira's wondering about getting a Mercedes,' Glenn said easily, 'so she thought she'd try mine out.'

'I thought you weren't going to drive again because of the crash,' Heather said as Kira pulled out into the traffic.

For the life of her Kira couldn't think of an answer. Again Glenn helped her out. 'That's quite a while ago now.'

'What did my teacher say?' Heather asked, a slight note of anxiety in her voice.

'That your maths is no good,' Glenn smiled.

Kira couldn't help but contrast his attitude with Stuart's. Had he been alive, Heather's result would now be the topic of a lengthy inquest, which doubtless was the reason the little girl had been so subdued this evening.

'I know,' she agreed dismally. 'I'm hopeless.'

'Uncle Glenn's promised to give you a hand so you'll do better next term,' Kira told her.

'Did it go all right, then? The open evening, I mean?' Heather asked, starting to brighten up.

'Of course it did,' Glenn said. 'Except you're to stop being so noisy in class.'

'I'm *not* noisy,' Heather protested, laughing.

Kira smiled. At this moment, with Glenn's straight-faced teasing, she was wondering how she had ever thought him to be austere.

She turned into the quiet avenue where she lived, the headlamps' white glare catching a cyclist in their steady beam. As she was about to pass him, he swerved a little and she caught her breath. Heather didn't even notice, but Glenn alongside her didn't miss her jumpy reaction.

As she pulled up outside her house she was shaking. She didn't feel she could get herself together immediately. Not wanting Heather to see what an ordeal driving home had been for her, she said, forgetting that it had been her intention in any case to give her and Glenn a chance to talk. 'Come in for coffee, Glenn.'

By the time she'd set the cups out in the kitchen and the kettle had boiled she felt calmer. She carried the tray into the drawing-room where Heather had set out the draughts board for a game with Glenn.

Kira sat back and watched while they played. She noticed the sure skill in Glenn's fingers as he moved the counters, the disturbingly attractive lines of his face in the muted lighting. Somehow she had never been aware of any man as she was of him.

As she looked at him, it flashed into her mind what it had been like to trace her hands over the hard muscles of his naked chest, to have his body everywhere around her. She fought to subdue it, but the stress of the drive had tired her and somehow she couldn't push from her thoughts the memory of his lovemaking. Their night together had affected her profoundly, but what had it meant to him?

Rather abruptly she said, 'If you've finished your hot milk, Heather, it's time for bed.'

Heather stared at the counters on the draughts board intently a moment before answering.

'OK,' she said, giving Glenn a mischievous smile. 'If I go on, Uncle Glenn's only going to beat me, so I'd rather stop now anyway.'

Glenn laughed and Heather came to Kira to kiss her goodnight. Kira hugged her close and her eyes followed the little girl with a smile as she left the room.

'You're very fond of Heather, aren't you?' Glenn commented as he stacked the draughtsmen in their box.

'Yes, I am,' she said. 'You seem very fond of her, too.'

'Well, that gives us something in common.'

She refused to be needled by his faint irony.

'You and I have got a lot in common,' she contradicted him, speaking calmly, though her heart was beginning to thump. 'You said not so long back that we didn't really know each other. You were right. But that's changed lately.'

Glenn leaned back in his chair. From his relaxation it appeared that she had not mentioned anything of particular importance. Yet there was a look of sharp attentiveness in his eyes as he asked leisurely, 'What specifically were you thinking of?'

It never occurred to her that she was being a hypocrite, seeking honesty from him about his feelings when she steadfastly refused to speculate on her own. She was too afraid of finding herself in love with a man who felt no more for her than sexual attraction. She knew what it was like to have affection returned half-heartedly. A sense of self-preservation made her determined not to discover the anguish of a love that was totally one-sided.

'We . . . we share a lot of interests,' she answered. Aware that Glenn was eyeing the nervous way she was using her hands to help express what she was trying to say, she promptly stilled them in her lap. 'We have the same friends, the same tastes. We even think alike when it comes to solving crosswords.'

'You've left out one important area where we also match up nicely,' Glenn mocked.

She had herself too tightly under control to rise to his deliberate provocation. A tinge of colour crept into her face, but her voice was as even as if she was confirming a clinical diagnosis.

'Yes,' she agreed. 'It also happens that we're sexually compatible.'

'It's certainly taken you a long enough to admit that.'

'Perhaps it has,' she parried. 'I . . . I was a bit shocked by what happened that night.'

There was a short silence and then Glenn enquired pleasantly, 'So what am I to make of your sudden discovery that we match up so well both in bed and out of it?'

Thrown on to the defensive, she fired back, 'I'm trying to find out what *you* make of it.'

Glenn kept his penetrating gaze on her while she glared back at him, refusing to divulge even a shadow of her thoughts. His eyes held a glint in their depths, but his voice had the same note of mockery as he asked, 'This isn't a leap year, is it?'

'What do you mean?' she asked shortly.

'I thought you were working up to a proposal.'

His laconic ridicule made her leap to her feet in a blaze of temper. Uncertain of her ground with him, she had had to steel herself to discuss their relationship, and the combination of strain and apparent rejection was more than she could endure.

'Propose to *you*?' she said with fury. 'We could have a century of leap years and I wouldn't propose to you!'

With predatory speed Glenn stood up, snatching hold of her by the forearms. She was too taken by surprise at his suddenness to offer even token resistance as he pulled her to his chest. There was more than a wintry grimness in his face , and her heart jolted with alarm as she recognised an anger even fiercer than her own.

'That was abundantly obvious,' he said in a suppressed voice that lashed her with its sarcasm. 'So why don't you tell me exactly what you *did* intend with all that talk about our relationship?'

'We don't have a relationship!'

His grip tightened and she shivered at the menacing chill in his blue eyes.

'If you're indulging in power games,' he said, his voice low and grating, 'expecting to prompt me into some kind of declaration of love, you'll be waiting a damned long time to hear it. I've let you get away with a lot. Evidently you've failed to realise that. But don't you ever behave with me like this again.'

He released her and she retreated quickly, afraid of finding herself inadvertently in his path as he strode from the room.

CHAPTER EIGHT

AWARE that she was trembling with reaction, Kira sank down in one of the nearest armchairs. The room seemed strangely still after their furious exchange. She ran her hand through her hair as, angrily, she puzzled over what he had meant by his last remark. Far from indulging in power games, she wasn't even sure she knew what they were!

And then, suddenly, she lifted her head with a quick jerk, dazed comprehension coming into her eyes. Glenn loved her and wanted her! It scarcely seemed possible, yet how else was she to interpret what he had said? He believed she had somehow guessed the strength of his feelings and was taking a cruel delight in the power it gave her over him. Didn't he know that the magnetism between them was a two-way force?

Her sense of wonder and joy was so intense, she was filled with impatience to set things right. Yet after their row she wasn't sure he was going to want to listen to her. Because of that, she waited a couple of days before phoning him.

Her heart was thudding crazily as she heard him pick up the receiver.

'Glenn? It's Kira,' she began, thankful that her voice sounded even.

'Hello, Kira. I'm afraid you've caught me on my way out. Is it important?'

It was, but his concise, business-like manner and the fact that he was in a hurry made her nerve falter about mentioning the other evening. She said instead, 'No, not especially. I wanted to talk to you, but it can wait.'

'In which case I'll call you back some time in the week.'

His dismissal was sufficiently offhand to set her mind clamouring with doubts. Wasn't she assuming an awful lot because of one heated remark? Wasn't she forgetting Clare, still somewhere in the equation?

When, after several days, Glenn finally called her at work, it was with the news that he was going to be away on business for the next fortnight. His voice held only the conventional amount of warmth and his manner was crisp. With no opportunity to say what she wanted, Kira was equally formal as she wished him a successful trip. Yet it wasn't until she received an invitation to June and Andy's barbecue that she began to feel that, far from being interested in her, Glenn was trying to loosen the ties between them.

Andy Fraser had been with the firm of accountants Stuart had set up from the early days. When Stuart had been alive Kira had done a lot of entertaining and the Frasers had been frequent visitors. Now she tended to see June mostly for the occasional coffee morning. Her friends had understood that for a time she hadn't wanted to be asked to small dinner parties.

But now she realised that rebuilding her life meant accepting invitations on her own. The Frasers' barbecue would be a good way to get back into circulation. It was Glenn, though, who clinched her decision. She knew he was certain to have been invited.

Before their last row he would undoubtedly have offered her a lift, and she would have relied on him to be an escort for the evening. The fact that he didn't phone her meant either that he had another engagement, or that he intended taking Clare. The suspicion alone made her furious. But at least by accepting the invitation she would find out at last where she stood with him.

She was still without a car. Since she'd driven home

at Glenn's insistance after Heather's school open evening she had enquired about both the Mercedes 190 and the Rover Sterling, but she hadn't yet made her final decision as to which she would buy. When it became obvious that Glenn wasn't going to get in touch with her, she arranged for a taxi to get to the Frasers'.

The evening was warm, so she chose a dress in turquoise and black cotton jersey. Gilt buttons on the bodice and a wide black belt gave it a slim, military chic. She hadn't realised till she was scarred from the crash how difficult it was to find a summer dress that wasn't cut to show off shoulders and neck. This one had a mandarin collar but left her arms completely bare.

She knew as she emphasised the allure to her eyes with dusky shadow and pinned her hair up sleekly that her aim was not only to stiffen her courage, but also to make Glenn appreciate what he had given up should he arrive at the barbecue with Clare.

The taxi dropped her a few yards from the Frasers' house for the kerb was packed with parked cars. As she walked towards the house she checked every one to see if it was Glenn's, but there was no silver-grey Mercedes. Her spirits lifted before she remembered that just because Glenn wasn't at the party with Clare didn't mean they weren't together somewhere else. The uncertainty he was putting her through was making her burn with a simmering resentment towards him.

June opened the door to her, looking smartly competent in a red sundress.

'Hello, Kira,' she carolled above the throb of the music. 'It's lovely to see you. Come on in.'

The house, with its modern split-level lounge, seemed full of noise and laughter. The french windows were open on to the patio and Kira could glimpse people, drinks in hand, chatting in groups. Coloured lights were strung down the long lawn and were already starting to glow more deeply, although it would be an hour or so till dusk fell. From the barbecue came the faint smell of charcoal.

Andy gave her a drink and she chatted to some of Stuart's friends she hadn't seen since the dinner dance, before going outside into the garden. If she couldn't actually enjoy the party, she was determined to put Glenn out of her thoughts.

She sat down on the stone wall that edged the patio, and looked down the well-tended garden as she sipped her martini. The evening breeze was warm after a beautiful day and the laughter and chatter had an indolent sound. Suddenly, against the muted background of music and conversation, she recognised the timbre of a man's voice.

She glanced round swiftly and then froze as she saw Glenn coming out through the french windows, his hand lightly guiding Clare. Kira's heart jolted with a mixture of shock and anguish. She realised she was gripping the stem of her glass almost tightly enough to snap it. She couldn't pretend she hadn't seen Glenn, for his gaze immediately alighted on her.

'Hello, Kira,' he began easily. 'I should have guessed you might be here.'

'Have you come alone?' Clare enquired sweetly.

'I'm afraid *you* booked my chauffeur for the evening,' Kira answered with an amused smile, pride lending her the bravado she needed.

A glint of cynical humour came into Glenn's eyes.

'I didn't think you needed a chauffeur these days,' he remarked.

'I don't,' she replied with the same lightly amused unconcern. 'Which is why I'm here alone.'

Her act was flawless, but it was one she felt could shatter with the slightest increase of pressure. She could have wept with chagrin at her naïveté in ever supposing that Glenn loved her. The recollection of how she had intended to put Clare in the shade was another lesson in stinging humiliation. Her dress, which had seemed perfect for the barbecue, looked prim beside Clare's black top and rustling short red skirt. Kira wore no necklace, but around Clare's throat was a heart-shaped locket, and her flawless shoulders glistened with a dusting of gold-flecked powder.

As they stood talking, Clare nestled against Glenn, tucking her hand through his arm in the silent assertion that she belonged to him. To watch her was a knife-thrust of pain and fury. Unable to endure any more, Kira said carelessly, 'I think I'll get another drink.'

She strolled leisurely across the patio, outwardly all poise and grace. No one would have guessed that her progress into the crowded lounge was a chaotic escape. Merely to remember now the night she had spent with Glenn made her feel cheap.

But if the evening had started off badly, worse was to follow. The lamplit patio, with its softly coloured shadows, was ideal for dancing, and as the night went on couples went out to dance to the soft, romantic music. Kira, feigning a vast interest in Andy's recent holiday in Tunisia, saw that among the couples moving together in a close embrace were Glenn and Clare. Suddenly she wished with a furious intensity that to save face she had asked Nigel to come with her. As she hadn't, she moved away to help June collect the used glasses, wondering just how soon she could decently leave.

When they were in the kitchen, June commented, 'I expected you and Glenn to come together.'

Was it merely an observation, or was June speculating about her relationship with him? Kira wondered. Did she suspect there had been something between them which was now over? Her pride had taken enough of a battering already without this, too. Angrily she told herself she was being touchy. But just the same she made sure she replied with complete disinterest.

'I understand Clare's an old university friend of his.'

'Andy tells me she talks nothing but money,' June remarked. 'I find it hard to believe she's as hard up as she makes out, considering the way she dresses.'

'Yes, she certainly has style,' Kira agreed, her smoke-screen of unconcern perfect.

She chatted with June as they washed up, hearing the sound of laughter from the lounge. As Kira rejoined the party she saw Glenn talking to another couple. His arm was casually around Clare's waist and, whatever joking exchange had just gone on, Clare seemed to be finding it helplessly amusing. She leaned her head against his shoulder before looking up at him with laughing eyes.

It was at that moment that inadvertently Kira's gaze locked with Glenn's. She swept him a faint, dismissive smile. A few moments ago she'd wanted nothing more than to leave. Now, tired of being cast as the woman alone, she was suddenly determined to prove to Glenn what a total irrelevancy he was in her life.

Without a partner it was obvious she wasn't going to dance, but she wasn't aiming to show him she was having a marvellous time. She intended establishing that she was serenely content talking quietly with Stuart's friends, that emotionally it was Stuart she was still tied to and that not by one strand was she linked to Glenn.

The effort of sustaining the illusion helped keep the pain round her heart in check. With iron will-power she refused to allow her eyes to stray in Glenn's direction again, though she did notice Clare saunter out later on to the patio, a bottle of Soave in one hand and a glass in the other.

Surreptitiously Kira glanced at her watch. She seemed to have done nothing but practise false smiles all evening. It wasn't yet eleven. If she was going to keep up this masterly pretence she needed a respite.

June had set one of the bedrooms aside as a cloakroom and Kira went upstairs, thankful to find that it was empty. The bright lighting in the tiled, en-suite bathroom made her look pale, and she paused in front of the vanity unit to renew her lipstick and to add a trace more blusher along her cheekbones. Her hair in its pretty chignon was still smooth, but she neatened it with her comb, noticing as she did so how dark her eyes had become.

She was wildly angry with Glenn. Tonight showed that he had used her as a one-night stand. She was in such a state of tempestuous fury that she would have loved to have stormed downstairs, slapped him in front of everyone and provoked a flaming row.

Yet her reflection gave no indication of her thoughts. Dark but steady amber eyes stared back at her. The bright lighting emphasised the coppery glints in her hair. As always, she looked graceful and calm. It had taken Glenn to recognise the embered sensuality beneath her calm assurance. But she was adamant that he'd never again spark her to either temper or passion. From now on she would treat him with a reserve more chilling than outright hate.

She had just gone back into the bedroom when Clare breezed in, blowing her jet-black fringe out of her eyes.

'It's so hot tonight,' she announced as she sat down at the dressing-table. She adjusted her low-cut bodice that showed off her luscious figure. Then with a little stab of *ingénue* maliciousness she asked, as she turned to look at Kira, 'Don't you find such a high collar uncomfortably warm? But then, of course, I forgot, you haven't been dancing.'

Immediately Kira's hand went to her throat. The crash meant that she would never again be able to wear a top like Clare's, and doubtless Clare had worked that out.

'I expect it's the wine that's made you hot,' she answered shortly.

Clare had gloated over her triumph and Kira had no intention of staying to receive more sweetly barbed comments. But as she went briskly to the door Clare delayed her by demanding, 'As Glenn is Heather's guardian, how much do you see of him?'

'Not all that much,' Kira answered carefully. In her temper she had forgotten what a threat Clare posed to her. 'Why do you ask?'

Clare shrugged and then said with a complacent little smile, 'I was just thinking that it's not a very satisfactory arrangement.'

'It's been very satisfactory till now,' Kira answered.

'Well, I think it would be much better if Heather was sent away to boarding-school. She'd learn independence.'

'What Heather needs most of all is stability,' Kira said sharply, trying to hold down a rising fear. 'Glenn and I are agreed on that.'

'Really?' Clare replied. 'Well, we'll see.'

She turned back to the dressing-table where she started to fluff up her curls with her fingers. Kira watched her for an instant. Then she went quickly out of the room, her mind racing.

Clare had made it clear that she was not going to allow Heather to form a bond between Glenn and another woman. Once the two of them were married she would see to it that his ward's home was no longer with Kira. The future couldn't be starker, yet still Kira refused to accept defeat.

Despite her position legally, she was adamant that she would not lose Heather without the most monumental struggle. Her determination calmed her a little. Later, somehow, she would think up a strategy, however desperate. But first she had to get through the rest of the evening.

As she went downstairs June was in the hall answering the phone.

'Kira,' she called. 'There's somebody asking for you.'

'For me?' Kira said, surprised, as she took the receiver.

June tactfully went back into the lounge as Kira took the call. It was Mrs Thorpe.

'Hello, Jean,' Kira said, catching the anxious note in her voice. 'Is everything all right?'

'Well, no, not really. I'm worried about Heather. She said she didn't feel very well earlier, but she didn't make much fuss and before she went to bed she said she felt a bit better. But now she's running a temperature and is complaining of very bad stomache ache. I expect it's just a tummy upset, so I haven't called the doctor, but she's very tearful . . .'

'I'll come home right away,' Kira said, interrupting her.

'I'm sorry to have to cut short your evening, but Heather did want me to phone. She wants you.'

'Tell her I'll be home just as soon as I can. I'll ring for a cab right now. Thanks, Jean. I'm glad you called.'

She rang off and immediately dialled for a taxi. She wasn't unduly worried about Heather and she was quite glad of the excuse to get away from the party. She found June in the kitchen and explained that she'd have to be leaving.

'Oh, poor Heather,' June said sympathetically. 'I do hope she'll soon feel better. Have you rung for a cab?'

'Yes, just now.'

'Well, I'm glad you could come,' June said, kissing her goodbye before hurrying back to her guests.

Kira wandered into the hall and then, glimpsing Glenn, retreated promptly into the kitchen, hoping he hadn't seen her. She was too late. He had.

Joining her, he asked, 'Are you leaving already?'

'Yes,' she said coldly. 'I have to. Jean's rung to say Heather's not well.'

'Can I run you home?' he offered.

'No,' she said, her eyes warring with him. 'I wouldn't want to spoil your evening.'

She'd meant her refusal to sound merely distant and polite. It came across as more pointed than that.

'Do I detect a note of jealousy?' Glenn mocked as he came towards her.

'I have no feelings for you, so why should I be jealous?' she said, fighting hard to maintain her icy poise. 'Your conceit, Glenn, is endless.'

'Then it's well matched by your repressed sexuality,' Glenn said.

There was a half-empty wine-glass on the work top beside her. Her temper, which had been simmering all evening, now came exploding to the surface. Impulsively she picked it up, about to throw the contents at him, but he anticipated her intention and grabbed hold of her wrist. The steely grip of his fingers forced hers open so that the glass toppled from her hand on to the worktop, the wine spilling harmlessly over the formica.

She gave a little gasp, and then, as he released her, she snatched her arm away defensively, rubbing her wrist. For an instant Glenn's eyes probed hers and then he walked out of the room.

She stood there, her head bowed. Never before had Glenn treated her rare displays of temper with such contemptuous indifference. On previous occasions there had been cynical amusement, anger, even a degree of male satisfaction in his eyes when he had finally succeeded in provoking her.

She felt chilled and humiliated. The taut undercurrents that had existed between them for so long seemed completely dead. He'd made her behave like a spitfire and then had snubbed her for her lack of restraint. God, he was loathsome.

The doorbell rang and, feeling close to stormy tears, she went out to her cab. The journey home passed her unnoticed. She was too preoccupied with thoughts of Glenn. She couldn't stop replaying the scene with him in the kitchen.

Why had he deliberately sought her out, and why had she, after keeping her cool all evening, let her rage get the upper hand? She wasn't the stereotypical red-head. She always thought before she acted, so why suddenly had she lost control? Yet deep down she knew why. Seeing him with Clare tonight had been more than she could stand.

She paid the taxi driver and hurried up the drive to her house. Jean came into the hall as she heard Kira's key in the door.

'How's Heather?' Kira began.

'She's not at all well,' Jean answered. 'She's just been sick again, though she'd had nothing to eat all evening.'

From upstairs Heather called plaintively, 'Is that you, Kira?'

'Yes, pet, it's me,' Kira called back as she went quickly upstairs.

She went into Heather's room. The little girl was lying in bed, her face wet with tears.

'I've got such bad tummy ache,' she whispered, her eyes huge with pain.

'Where?' Kira asked gently. 'Can you tell me where?'

'It's everywhere,' Heather sobbed pathetically. 'All over my tummy.'

The suspicion was already forming in Kira's mind that this was something more serious than a bug. Heather's symptoms sounded very much like appendicitis, especially when taken together with her stomach pains on the evening of Kira's theatre trip with Nigel. She must have had a grumbling appendix then.

'I think I'm going to get the doctor to have a look at you,' she said, giving Heather a reassuring smile.

She went to smooth the covers more neatly, but

Heather whimpered instantly, 'Don't touch the duvet. It hurts too much.'

Jean was hovering in the doorway. As Kira joined her on the landing, she said, her voice low and anxious, 'I wasn't sure whether or not to phone you. But Heather's never made a fuss like this before.'

At well past eleven on a Saturday night it wasn't easy to get hold of a doctor. Jean had at last gone home and Kira sat waiting with Heather. The little girl tossed and moaned while Kira tried to soothe her. She hated seeing Heather so ill, and being able to do nothing to make her feel better.

When the doorbell finally rang, she started, her nerves rubbed raw. The doctor, a young man in his twenties, was friendly and kind with Heather. He confirmed what Kira had been afraid of. Heather was suffering from acute appendicitis and needed to be admitted to hospital immediately.

For Kira the night was starting to seem endless. After the doctor had gone she quickly started packing Heather's nighties and sponge bag. It wasn't till she had put everything ready and was waiting for the ambulance to arrive that she realised that *she* couldn't sign the consent form for the operation Heather needed. Glenn would have to sign.

She had never been so furious with Stuart as she was at that moment. Her stepdaughter needed an emergency operation and *she* couldn't give permission for it to take place! It had to be Glenn.

Quickly she dialled his number. She expected it to ring a little time on account of the hour, but when he still didn't pick it up she began to get alarmed. Where on earth could he be?

And then, with untempered fury, she knew the answer. He was with Clare. Angrily she seized the phone book, before realising she didn't know Clare's surname. She fought against a sharp uprise of panic.

Delay now could mean peritonitis might develop. And then she remembered that, as Clare was an employee of Stuart's firm, Andy was likely to have her number.

To have to ask him in order to contact Glenn was the final humiliation of the evening. Worried about Heather, her temper rose yet another notch at the deftness with which Glenn had embarrassed her tonight. She called Andy and then, having obtained the number, she dialled Clare's home.

It was the most difficult phone call she had ever made. It was quickly answered by Clare. Keeping her voice calm and impersonal, Kira began, 'Hello, Clare. It's Kira Newall. I'm trying to get hold of Glenn. It's very urgent.'

There was a hostile pause and then Clare said with cool unfriendliness, 'Well, you've tracked him down. He's here.' She heard the receiver being put down and then Clare's voice, faint but perfectly audible announce, 'It's Kira. That redhead can't seem to leave you alone.'

Then Glenn, as authoritative as ever, came on the line.

'Hello, Kira. What's happened? Is Heather OK?'

How the hell could he sound so natural when she had interrupted him with Clare? Were they at this moment in bed together? Had he had to lean over her to pick up the receiver? For an instant her throat felt so tight she couldn't speak. She must not break down. The years of hospital training took over.

'Heather's got acute appendictis,' she managed tautly. 'She's being taken into St Hero's, but before she can have the operation your signature's needed.'

'I'll be straight there,' Glenn said, before adding, 'She'll be all right, Kira.'

'I don't need your platitudes,' she flared. 'Just when I need you, where the hell are you? God knows why Stuart made you Heather's guardian!'

'Save the accusations,' Glenn ordered, cutting her

short. More gently he went on. 'I know you're worried about Heather, but appendicitis isn't a serious operation today. I'll be at the hospital in about fifteen minute. Now keep calm.'

'And don't you tell me to keep calm!' she stormed before slamming the phone down.

Yet he did keep her calm. Once he had arrived at the hospital he took over, signed the necessary form and reassured Kira throughout the long wait for news. She sat in the waiting-room, cramped with worry. She remembered from her training one of the doctor's words. 'Every anaesthetic carries with it a risk.' Why did she have to remember them so clearly now? She started as Glenn took her hand in his, and in the agony of the moment she let him draw her wordlessly into his arms.

It was seven o'clock in the morning when Heather came back from the recovery-room. She was still not fully round from the anaesthetic, and the nurse on duty suggested they come back later in the morning.

The roads were wide and empty and Sunday-morning still as Glenn drove her home. An immense relief and thankfulness filled her after the ordeal of the long night. She glanced at Glenn, seeing that his jaw was shadowed.

She remembered the last time she had seen the strong lines of his face made more rugged by a night's growth of beard. She didn't feel appalled now by the fact that she had slept with him. She felt too desperately tired, as though she had no emotions left, leaving her curiously detached.

All night she'd endured the knowledge that it was a possibility that Heather could die. Now she was facing up to a different kind of fear, that she would lose her because of Clare. With Clare as her stepmother the child's life would be a misery. Except that wasn't going to happen. With sudden clarity Kira knew she had her strategy.

Glenn had wanted her once, albeit for only one night, and she was going to make him want her again. She'd never before set out deliberately to entice a man, but she was going to do it now. Quite how, she wasn't sure, not because she had any scruples, but because what she wanted from Glenn was nothing less than marriage.

She refused to consider how pathetically slim her chance of success was. Heather was worth the risk of a jeering rejection. She knew Glenn wasn't in love with her, but not until he told her in so many words would she believe he loved Clare. He might be emotionally involved with Clare, but not to the extent of being in love—not yet. Kira didn't question how she was so sure of that. She simply knew it with a woman's under-standing she would not doubt for fear of losing her courage.

As they neared her house she broke the silence by saying, 'Come in and have breakfast with me. Please, I'd rather not be alone.'

She realised that if she intended playing the temptress she'd have to sound more relaxed.

'You know me too well to have to say please,' Glenn said, flicking a glance at her.

'Do you intend all your remarks to have a double meaning?' she asked with a spark of hostility.

'What's wrong, Kira?' he mocked softly. 'Can't you forget the night we spent together?'

With a sense of dangerous triumph she realised that a bond of curbed animosity was still there between them. More sure of herself she countered, 'Can you?'

Glenn drew up outside her house, his eyes deliberately raking her.

'Are you sure you want me to answer that?' he said softly.

She was about to give him an angry glare and then

she remembered her intention. Sweeping him a sultry glance, she got out of the car. Glenn's footsteps sounded close behind her on the gravel drive. She wondered nervously if she really knew what she was doing, but her determination not to lose Glenn never wavered. Her fingers were unsteady with the key, and he took it from her and unlocked the front door himself.

'I'm sorry,' she laughed. 'I seem to be terribly on edge.'

'It's been a long night,' said Glenn. 'It's reaction.'

'I suppose so,' she agreed, reaching up a hand to unpin her chignon.

Her bright hair tumbled around her shoulders. She ran her fingers through it, searching for loose pins, knowing that the gesture was provocative. She wasn't sure if it was apprehension that was making her heart beat faster. Glenn's eyes were unreadable as they met hers, but his jaw was set tight and she had a stab of satisfaction that, if nothing else, she was starting to needle him.

'What would you like for breakfast?' she asked. 'Can I cook you something? I've eggs and bacon in the fridge.'

'Such hospitality,' he remarked. 'What's the motive, Kira?'

She felt herself colour. For an instant she had the awful impression that he'd guessed exactly what she was up to. Her eyes defied his as she said icily, 'Tonight's shown me that, for Heather's sake, it's vital that we get along. But if you can't accept an olive branch when it's offered then perhaps it would be better if you left.'

Glenn's blue eyes mocked her as he said, 'Are you suggesting that we kiss and make up?'

'I wouldn't have put it in quite those terms,' she said, her heart fluttering. 'But yes, that is the general idea.'

He laughed, but there was something harsh in the sound and quickly she lowered her gaze, afraid of what she was doing. She'd meant to be sweet and enticing, but somehow the vibrations between them were making it difficult. She was quite convinced that a show of feminine charm would have had a man like Nigel quickly captivated, but with sudden comprehension she knew that Glenn wouldn't be satisfied with a superficial pretence. He'd stirred her to reckless passion before and he wouldn't be deceived by anything else. She was playing with fire and an instinctive sense of caution made her revert to coolness with him.

Over breakfast she was glad to keep their conversation innocuous. Mostly they talked of Heather. With a sinking feeling of dismay Kira started to wonder if she really could get what she wanted from Glenn. She could imagine what strain and sleeplessness had done for her looks, and the cold light of morning wasn't the best time to remind him of what they were like together. Clare, with her smouldering charm, was formidable competition. The challenge stiffened Kira's spirit. She wasn't going to lose her nerve now.

She patted a yawn and stretched, raising her graceful arms and arching her supple body.

'I can't seem to wake up,' she remarked with a sleepy smile.

She saw Glenn's eyes glint and felt a shiver of dangerous anticipation. But it was short-lived, for he pushed his coffee-cup aside and said, 'Get some rest and then give me a ring when you want to go back to the hospital. I'll drive you.'

His impersonal generosity goaded her to recklessness. She knew he was aware of her as a women and she didn't want either kindness or concern from him. She wanted a simmering antagonism between them that would ultimately shatter into a blaze of passion.

'I'll get Nigel to take me,' she said, 'but thanks for the offer.'

Glenn frowned.

'Nigel? I thought you'd finished with him.'

'You mean you thought you'd driven him away,' she said, looking at him with veiled hostility. 'Well, tonight's made me realise I need someone for support, someone to lean on in a crisis.'

'Then at least pick a man, not a smooth . . .'

'Don't insult my friends,' she cut across him, getting swiftly to her feet. 'Let me tell you something, Glenn. I'm tired of having to be grateful to you and I'm damned if I'm going to have you treat me as an incompetent nuisance any longer.'

'Incompetent, perhaps,' Glenn mocked as he stood up. 'A nuisance—never.'

'Save your sense of humour for your flamboyant girl-friend,' she said with the frosty hauteur she knew maddened him. 'Maybe she'll appreciate it.'

She got no further. Glenn swore savagely under his breath and snatched her into his arms. She felt a moment's shock of pure exultant pleasure. And then her arms went up around his neck, her lips parting willingly to the fierce invasion of his kiss.

Her heart was beating with a quickness that made her feel almost faint. Glenn kissed her long and relentlessly, and she leaned into his strong, lean body, answering him with an ardent passion. When finally he raised his head she was weak with desire and a heady sense of triumph. She saw that he was breathing as fast as she was, and the knowledge of what it had been like before, when he had taken complete possession of her, heightened her sense of reckless excitement.

'Glenn,' she whispered huskily as he claimed her mouth again.

Instinctively her hand slid into the thick hair at the nape of his neck. She could feel the roughness of his face against her skin as he kissed her till a wild, melting pleasure ran like intoxicating liquor through her blood. Her body had come alive at his touch. Shocked at how rapidly he was arousing her, she tried to cling on to sanity, to remember why she had started this, but instead she lost to the demands of his mouth and his knowing hands.

She felt his fingers stroke the softness of her breast and she clutched at his shoulders, almost alarmed at the driving need he was stirring in her. He ran his thumb over her tautly aroused nipple, and she gave a low moan of bewildered, aching pleasure before, almost roughly, he tilted her chin up and demanded raggedly, 'Look at me, Kira.'

Slowly she opened her eyes, allowing him to see the depth of desire in them.

'You witch,' he breathed, his hand stroking the graceful curve of her throat, his fingers pausing to press lightly against her pulse points that throbbed feverishly with excitement.

'Kiss me,' she whispered.

She trembled as his mouth found hers again in a ravaging kiss. Glenn slid his hand down her spine, pressing her hips to his. The throb of his masculinity possessed her with a need to feel his body a part of hers. He gave a low growl in his throat as his hands dealt swiftly with the buttons of her bodice and then slid possessively over her breast.

At the back of her mind was the vague notion of some purpose that she had now forgotten. But her world was too dark and dizzy for her to recall anything but the fact that, for whatever reason, she had wanted this to happen and that it was right to surrender to this engulfing vortex of longing.

She felt him swing her off her feet and sanity returned a little as he carried her into the drawing-room and lowered her on to the sofa. His hard body leant over hers as he eased the neckline of her dress away to give his mouth access to the nipples his hands had already tantalised and caressed.

'I want to look at you,' he murmured huskily.

The morning light in the room was harsh and bright, and in a defensive panic she pushed frantically at him.

'No,' she gasped. 'Please! Don't!'

She had started to struggle wildly. Glenn raised his head, his face flushed under his tan, his breathing ragged. She sat up, hurriedly buttoning her dress with trembling fingers. Her skirt had ridden up to her thighs and she was about to smooth it when Glenn caught hold of her by the shoulders, forcing her to face him.

'Just what are you playing at?' he demanded angrily.

Her fear of rejection if he saw in broad daylight how badly scarred she was faded, as her dazed mind recalled why she had allowed him to kiss and caress her this way. Her eyes were dark as she said unsteadily, 'I'm not playing. I want to know if you still want me.'

A savage gleam came into his eyes. He put a finger under her chin and tilted her face up.

'Are you leading me on, sweetheart? If so, it's a dangerous game to play.'

'I'm not leading you on,' she said, her heart jolting.

'What, then?' he demanded gratingly as she stumbled to her feet and twisted her hair into a knot from her flushed face.

For an instant she didn't think she could force herself to say the words. Then she turned back, her voice a throaty whisper as she began, 'I want us to get married.'

Something leapt in the depths of Glenn's eyes, but she was too beside herself to notice. If he rejected her, everything would be over. It would be a prelude to her whole life collapsing in ruins. Curling her hands into fists, she rushed on huskily, 'We . . . we've been friends for a long time and we both know what we want in a partner. We've already discovered we share companionship and that as lovers we're compatible. You were the most loyal friend Stuart could have had. I know if we were married you'd be true to me . . . and there would be nothing I wouldn't do to try and make our marriage happy . . .'

To her dismay, even while she was speaking, she found that her vision had blurred with tears. Immediately Glenn was beside her. Sobbing, she tried to push him away, certain that he was going to jeer at her, and more vulnerable than she had ever been in all her life.

But Glenn was having none of her resistance. Taking hold of her firmly he tilted her chin up, staring into her eyes that were magnified by tears she was powerless to control. Her self-possession and her pride were in shreds. She couldn't even find a last reserve of strength to fight him.

'Just when I decide I've finally got you worked out, you set me wondering all over again,' he said speculatively.

Distraught, she flashed back, her voice cramped with anguish, 'Don't . . . don't think you have to soften what you're going to say. You . . . you think it's a damned fool idea.'

'On the contrary,' he said, gentle laughter in his voice. 'I think it's the most sensible idea you've come up with in a long while.'

She gazed at him, stupefied with disbelief. He had snatched her out of such a wilderness of pain and bleakness, she could scarcely comprehend it all at once.

'You mean . . .' she faltered.

'I think marriage is the only answer for you and me,' he said with a touch of humour as he brushed a tear away from her cheek with a deft, caressing finger.

His tenderness, coupled with her growing dazed happiness, made her incapable of answering for an instant. Everything was starting to seem slightly unreal. Far more calmly than she felt, she agreed, 'Yes . . . I think it is.'

Glenn looked at her closely, his eyes sharp. She couldn't read his thoughts but she didn't care. The imperturbable way he had met her suggestion was nothing short of astonishing, but she certainly wasn't going to question it.

He took hold of her left hand, which showed the diamond solitaire and platinum wedding ring Stuart had given her.

'What are you doing?' she asked.

'Now that we're engaged,' he answered as he removed her rings and set them aside, 'you don't need these.' He slipped the gold signet ring he wore off his hand and put it on her engagement finger. 'I don't want you, when you've caught up on some sleep, to think this was all a dream. Heather's given you a scare and, as you said, you need someone to lean on. But that doesn't mean you're entitled to second thoughts when you feel calmer.'

The words were said with a smile, but there was no doubting the firmness behind them. For once, with no wish to be defiant, she answered, 'I'm not going to change my mind. I intend marrying you.'

He cupped her face with his hands, looking down at her for what seemed a long time before bending to her mouth. She melted against him, surprised and disappointed when instead of prolonging the embrace he set her free. Dropping one more kiss lightly on her lips, he said, 'Get some rest and I'll call for you at eleven.'

She stayed where she was for some time after she'd heard the front door close. Then she lifted her hand to look at Glenn's heavy signet ring on her engagement finger. She couldn't work out why he had agreed to her suggestion, and at present she felt too bewildered to even try.

Her eyes strayed to the silver-framed photograph of Stuart that stood on the piano. Quickly she walked over to it and abruptly turned the photo face-down. She had been driven by desperation into asking Glenn to marry her because she was afraid of losing Heather. But the interrupting thought, too quick to be suppressed, was that she had done it also for herself.

CHAPTER NINE

WHEN Glenn and Kira returned to the hospital Heather was awake. She looked very pale, but she wasn't in any pain, and although she soon tired she didn't want Kira and Glenn to leave. Wincing as she moved, she propped herself up more comfortably on the pillows.

'I feel better now I'm wearing my own nightie and not that horrid white thing with strings down the back,' she said.

'It wasn't very glamorous,' Kira laughed.

'Well,' Glenn remarked teasingly to Heather, 'you stood up pretty well to the shock of the op. Now let's see how you stand up to a bit of news Kira and I have got for you.'

Kira's eyes met his in a conspiratorial glance. She had never felt so happy and at ease with him, nor seen him in such a relaxed mood.

'What is it?' Heather asked, smiling. 'Is it nice?'

'When you come back from Canada, how would you like to live with both of us?'

'Do you really mean it?' Heather exclaimed excitedly. 'That would be super. Are you getting married?'

'Yes, Glenn and I have decided to get married,' Kira laughed.

'When's the wedding going to be?' Heather asked eagerly.

'As soon as you're well again,' Glenn told her. 'We want it before you leave for Canada.'

Kira, still marvelling that he had accepted her proposal, was surprised that he intended them to be married so quickly. As they left the ward together at the end of visiting time, she said, 'You certainly don't believe in long engagements.'

'Not with someone as unpredictable as you,' he said, gently teasing her back.

'I'm not unpredictable,' she protested with a laugh, slipping her arm through his quite naturally before she'd even thought.

Glenn promptly drew her closer. Smiling down at her, he said, 'Together with your waywardness, it's part of your charm. Now, where do you fancy going for lunch?'

The tender rapport between them enfolded her in an aura of quiet joy. She couldn't make sense of it, but so long as the enchantment didn't shatter she felt she wouldn't care if she never made sense of anything ever again. Kissing his arm impulsively, she said, 'I'll leave it to you. I'm in the mood for a mystery tour.'

They had lunch in a smart restaurant in a picturesque village on the Thames. Afterwards they strolled along the towpath until it broadened out into gently rolling meadow. The sun was bright and hot, and few river-craft passed to disturb the hypnotic stillness. Swallows swooped and darted over the water, while away from the meandering river a patchwork of fields merged into the hilly distance to meet a hazy blue sky.

Having walked far enough, they stretched out on the parched grass. Glenn lay back, his hands clasped behind his head while Kira closed her eyes, feeling the sun warm on her skin. The crickets chirped in the dry grass and faintly in the distance came the throb of a river cruiser. She sighed, knowing a contentment she had not felt in years.

'What's the matter?' Glenn murmured drowsily as he ran his palm in a reassuring caress up her bare arm.

'Nothing,' she breathed with a smile, her voice trailing off sleepily. 'Not one single thing.'

When she woke and opened her eyes it was to find

herself looking into Glenn's steady blue gaze. He was lying beside her in complete relaxation, propped up on one elbow as though he had been watching her for some time as she slept. The eye-contact between them was so powerful, it sent a shiver of anticipation through her, quickening her breathing.

A faint smile softened the lines of Glenn's swarthy, trenchant face. Still with no words spoken between them, he tucked a silky strand of hair behind her ear before leaning over her. His body scarcely grazed hers as supporting himself on his forearm he bent to kiss her, yet the touch of his lips as they claimed hers made a current as potent as mead heat her blood. She kissed him back, her senses reeling with the heady pleasure of the lingering sweetness of his mouth on hers.

When finally his lips left hers he lay back, expelling his breath with a soft, muffled groan she had no difficulty in interpreting. Her pulse racing, she raised herself to look at him. Immediately he caught hold of her wrist, tugging her on top of him. Colour came into her face as her thigh was brought into contact with his and her breast softly crushed against his chest. She knew he must be able to feel the wild beating of her heart, yet, she had no more inclination to pull away than he had to release her.

'What happened between you and Nigel?' he asked, brushing her lips lightly with his forefinger.

Ensnared by his gaze she said softly, 'You *know* what happened. You drove him away.'

'He gave up that easily?' Glenn said with a trace of provoking humour.

She laughed and answered, 'You have to admit the set-up in the house that night did look a little unconventional. Nigel obviously wondered just what our relationship was.'

Glenn's eyes were intent on her face as he said, 'You could always have spelled it out for him.'

'No, I couldn't,' she said, drawing away from him and sitting back on her heels. 'I couldn't because I didn't know.' She dropped her gaze, not nearly sure enough of him to admit that even now that they were engaged she still didn't know what to make of their relationship. Instead she said with a touch of her old antagonism, 'After all, at the time we weren't friends exactly, were we?'

'No,' Glenn agreed drily, amused. 'It was certainly more complicated than that.' He got to his feet, pulling her up with him as he said, a slightly husky note to his voice, 'But I think we've spent enough time discussing the two of us here by the river. Idyllic though it is, it's too public for the sort of communication I have in mind.'

Concern came into her eyes. Baldly she said, 'No, Glenn. I . . . I can't.'

He did not seem as surprised by her statement as she might have expected. His face was impassive. Only the tightening of his cheek muscles showed he was tense in some way.

'I didn't notice any objection when I was making love to you a few minutes ago.'

'I know, but . . .' She couldn't have explained even if she'd wanted to. Events had moved far too swiftly for her to have even attempted to sort out her feelings. All she knew was that despite the way her senses stirred at his touch she wasn't ready to go to bed with him right now. She needed to learn to trust him before she could give herself to him completely. Now the only reason she could manage to voice was, 'I . . . I didn't sleep with Stuart until after we were married, and although I know I . . .'

Quizzical amusement came into his eyes as she stumbled to a halt. Scanning her face, he said, 'Are you trying to tell me that despite our night together you're the old-fashioned type who doesn't believe in sex before marriage?'

With a slight lift of her chin she answered, 'Yes. I . . . I suppose I am.'

Glenn gave a short sigh, the expression that crossed his face indecipherable. But there was no mistaking the note of wry humour in his voice as he remarked, 'Then it's just as well I said that ours would be a short engagement.'

She had no doubts about how strongly he desired her, but at that moment she was too profoundly grateful for his calm acceptance of what she'd said to want to question him about it.

They visited the hospital again during the evening, and Kira was pleased to see how much brighter Heather was. She was struck by the notion of how much like a family the three of them seemed, and then tensed with the thought. Until that instant it hadn't crossed her mind that she should tell Glenn it was a possibility that she couldn't have children. She felt sudenly cold, engulfed by a sense of inadequacy.

How could she steel herself to confess to him that she had doubts about her fertility? Suppose this altered everything? She couldn't bear to see the happiness of today shattered into a myriad irretrievable pieces. And yet she knew she couldn't not tell him. Caring about him far more deeply than she chose to acknowledge, she had to be honest with him, whatever it cost her.

She fought to pull herself together and to behave naturally and not as if she was on the brink of a calamity. Heather settled down sleepily for the night and, kissing her goodbye, Kira left the hospital with Glenn. She caught the glance he slanted her as they crossed the car park in relative silence, and quickly averted her gaze to escape his scrutiny. She didn't want him to guess how anxious her thoughts were.

'Would you like to come back to my place for a drink, or would you prefer it if I dropped you straight home?'

he asked as he started the ignition.

'I'd like to come home with you.'

'Is this your way of telling me you've changed your mind about sleeping with me?' he mocked gently.

Thoroughly on edge, there was moment's flash of anger in her eyes. Bringing her temper in check, she answered coolly, 'I thought I'd make myself clear on that point. I just want to talk to you.'

Glenn gave her a swift, probing look, but made no comment. Instead he kept the conversation matter-of-fact. She found her gaze straying to his profile, pain tightening round her heart as she tried desperately to summon up the sort of courage she would need to make her confession. Trying to match his manner imposed yet a further element of strain on her.

'What will you have to drink?' he asked when they'd arrived at his house.

'I'll have a brandy,' she said tersely.

'What exactly have you got to tell me that you need a brandy?'

She didn't answer. Conscious of his astute level gaze on her she accepted the glass he handed to her.

'You're not pregnant, are you, Kira?'

She glanced up sharply.

'No!' she denied, colour coming into her face at his reminder of how recklessly she had behaved that night.

'It was just a thought,' he said evenly, dismissing her indignation. 'I wondered if it might have been the reason for your sudden desire to be married. What is it, then?'

She hesitated, and then stood up and paced nervously towards the french windows. To lose him to Clare now would be more than she could bear. In a rush she began, 'Do . . . do you want children, Glenn?'

'Yes,' he answered, his voice level, though he was watching her with eyes that were as sharp as a hunter's. 'I assumed you did, too.'

'I do,' she agreed, unable to meet his eyes and rigid with tension. 'But . . . but I'm not sure I can have any.'

'Is this your way of wriggling out of our engagement?' he asked, his voice becoming brutal.

It had been pure hell to begin this, and his distrust and lack of belief made her flare into stormy anger.

'No, damn you, it isn't!' she exclaimed, her voice rising. 'I thought you had a right to know. You said you wanted me. Well, maybe I'm barren, so perhaps you don't any more.'

She broke off for she hadn't intended using such a dramatic word. She knew it conveyed more than sincerity. It showed real desperation, doubts about herself as a woman, and she wished fervently she hadn't used it.

Glenn came towards her and took the brandy glass out of her hands and set it aside.

'What makes you think you can't have children?' he asked, his voice suddenly quiet and strangely gentle. 'Have you had tests?'

She was used to medical frankness, but to talk to Glenn about her problems with conceiving made her feel sensitive and raw. Medical discussions were generally impersonal. What she and Glenn were talking about now was whether she would ever be pregnant by him.

'I hoped tests wouldn't be necessary,' she said in a cramped voice as she moved away a little. 'I . . . I know they can be quite an ordeal, and Stuart and I had only been trying for a year.'

'But you want a baby,' Glenn said.

'Yes,' she whispered, turning back to him.

'Then if there are doubts about your conceiving it would make sense not to use protection when we start making love.'

The conversation was fast becoming more than she could handle. All she could do was nod. Glenn came nearer and tilted her chin up, his blue eyes holding her captive. Softly he said, 'If frequency of making love will make you pregnant, you'll have a child before a year's over, Kira, I promise you.'

Although there were no questions in her mind about what she was doing, Kira found the days leading up to the wedding a strain. She was no nearer to learning why Glenn had decided to marry her, but she remembered only too clearly what it was like when love wasn't equally reciprocated. Yet she knew without a qualm that Glenn would respect her and be loyal to her. That, together with safeguarding her stepdaughter's happiness, would have to satisfy her.

The wedding had been arranged so that they would be back from their long weekend honeymoon in Paris in time to see Heather off on her trip to Canada. The little girl was excited and interested in every detail of the wedding plans. She admired Kira's choice of simple cream suit and sling-back shoes. Together they decided on a spray of bud carnations and tea roses to be worn on the jacket's lapel, and Heather insisted on a frivolous wisp of net and cream ribbon for Kira's chestnut hair.

'You're going to look beautiful,' Heather exclaimed. 'And I'm going to take hordes of photos so I can show all my friends when I go back to school.'

It was an ideal opening for Kira to talk to Heather about her marriage. Her stepdaughter had seemed thrilled by the idea from the outset, but Kira was still a little anxious about yet another upheaval in Heather's life. Her parents' divorce and then losing her mother had been behind her stammering problems when she'd first been referred to Kira at the age of four for therapy. Whatever Kathryn's faults, it seemed she'd been a loving parent and Heather had been horribly confused by the divorce proceedings. Kira needed to know positively that she had no suppressed doubts or anxieties about her marrying Glenn.

'I know planning a wedding is fun,' she began, 'but things will be completely different once I'm married. It won't be just you and me any more living in our old house.'

'I like Uncle Glenn's house better,' Heather announced. 'And anyway, I wouldn't mind where we lived so long as we were all together. I've . . .'

She broke off and Kira prompted, 'You've what?'

'Well . . . I've sort of hoped you and Uncle Glenn would get married one day. That was why I didn't like it when you went out with Nigel. You see, I wanted Uncle Glenn to be my dad in the same way that you're sort of my mother.'

It was an emotional moment for Kira. Hugging Heather, she said huskily, 'I just wanted you to be sure, honey.'

'Of course I'm sure,' Heather answered.

Kira found the little girl's excitement infectious, despite her vague uneasiness about what she was committing herself to. It didn't help that she knew instinctively that Stuart would have hated the idea of her marrying Glenn. Although he'd claimed him as his closest friend, Stuart had always been fiercely competitive and it had pleased him, she suspected, that she'd been reserved and a shade cool with Glenn. She felt somehow that she was betraying Stuart's trust, and yet she had to be sensible. She had loved Stuart while he was alive, but now she had to do what was best for her and Heather.

The thought made her heart race a little with apprehension. At times she was afraid that Glenn with his penetrating mind, would suspect that she was marrying him to stop Clare taking Heather from her. And, if he ever should guess, what would be his reaction?

And yet, strangely, despite being nervous, she enjoyed the wedding. It was a most beautiful languid

summer's day, and the register office brought no
stabbing reminders of her marriage to Stuart, which
had been a much grander and more formal affair.

The reception was held at a country hotel on the
fringes of London. As they drove there after the quiet
ceremony Glenn commented, 'Well, the knot's been
tied. You're mine now, Kira;'

He had never struck her as a possessive man, but
there was unmistakable possessiveness in his statement
and again she felt a twist of unease. She had already
made up her mind that she would never let herself love
any man the way she have loved Stuart. It left her too
exposed and vulnerable. Yet just how much did Glenn
intend demanding from her in their relationship? she
wondered, and she was glad of the laughter and light-
heartedness of the reception to divert her thoughts.

The hotel was set in extensive grounds overlooking
sloping countryside. Glenn's sisters' children played on
the lawns with Beth's three and Heather. Mrs Thorpe
couldn't resist saying as she watched them that soon
Glenn's parents would have more delightful grand-
children. Glenn pulled Kira close and brushed her
temple with his lips, sending her a tacit message of
reassurance as he laughed good-temperedly, 'We don't
intend letting you down on that score.'

The speeches were brief. Kira was touched by the
telegram her father had sent. At such short notice it
hadn't been possible for him to be at the wedding, but
his love and good wishes meant a lot to her. Then came
the cutting of the cake, with Glenn's tanned hand
covering hers. Her eyes met his and she smiled,
conscious of a strange sense of closeness which she was
suddenly convinced she could build on to make a
strong and happy marriage.

It seemed no time after that before they were being
showered with confetti as they got into Glenn's
Mercedes for the drive to Heathrow. Heather, who was

going to stay with Beth, waved them off vigorously, and Kira turned as Glenn pulled away to wave back to her and to the group of friends and in-laws who stood to see them off.

They stopped at the end of the long drive and Glenn said with an amused smile, 'If I know those nephews of mine, we're bound to have a "Just Married" sign on the bumper at the very least.'

She laughed. The feeling of fun was all around her, strengthened by the champagne she had drunk for the toasts. Turning to him, she put her palm against his jaw and kissed him with her first real display of loving affection. When she drew back, he was watching her closely. But almost immediately the intent look faded from his eyes, and with a smile he took her hand. At that moment she had no doubts that everything was going to be all right.

Their hotel in Paris was in the Premier Arrondissement, and Glenn had timed their arrival so that after freshening up they could have dinner. The restaurant, with its stately cream and gilt décor, was spacious and elegant and the service unhurried and solicitous.

Kira found she had little appetite, though the food was excellent. Her mood of happy confidence had ebbed and she glanced a shade apprehensively at Glenn as he refilled her wine-glass, unable to subdue her awareness of his strong, knowing hands. Not once during their three weeks engagement had either of them mentioned Clare. Kira was too certain that her husband didn't love her to want to ask him his motives for marrying her. She assumed he needed her in some way, and it was obvious from their quiet moments together that he desired her.

A panicky feeling took hold of her about what she had committed herself to. Her husband no longer seemed the amusing, urbane man she had shared laughter with at the reception. He was back to being the implacable outsider who for so long had been her enemy and whose gold wedding ring now bound her to him.

When she declined a dessert from the sweet trolley, he commented as though he read her mind, 'Don't tell me you're suffering from wedding-night nerves. You're no novice, Kira, to the delights of the bedroom.'

'I'm a little tired, that's all,' she answered defensively. 'It's been a long day.'

Glenn's eyes held hers for a moment before travelling to her mouth and then the curve of her throat.

'You'll be even more tired in a while,' he said softly, 'for it's going to be an even longer night.'

His face was serious and his words unmitigated by any of their usual humour.

'You really expect your pound of flesh, don't you?' she snapped.

His eyes hardened.

'That's a strange remark for a bride to make to her husband on their wedding night,' he said with cutting sarcasm.

'Forget I said it,' she said hurriedly. 'I don't know what I meant by it, anyway.'

'I think you do,' he contradicted, his eyes locking with hers. 'I expect everything from you that a woman can give to a man. You know that, and it bothers you, doesn't it?'

'I'll give you what I can and no more,' she answered defiantly and, leaving him to finish his brandy, she went up to their bedroom.

It was an inauspicious beginning. She got ready for bed and then sat at the dressing-table, rhythmically brushing her hair as she tried to unwind. Yet she could not relax. When Glenn had first made love to her she had experienced with him a transcendence and a breaking of bonds she had never known before. She was afraid of the elemental woman he brought out in her. She had to safeguard her emotional sovereignty, and yet, with the response he demanded from her, how could she?

She set the brush down with a slight clatter as Glenn came into the room. Almost defensively she stood up, seeing his eyes travel over her white broderie anglaise nightgown that with the lamplight behind her had acquired a beguiling transluscence. His eyes were dark and in his smart suit he looked disturbingly urbane, with a virile, threatening masculinity.

He came towards her and drew her into his arms.

'You look as if no man's ever touched you,' he murmured huskily.

His hands explored her nakedness beneath the fine material as he kissed her, and she felt the tremor of restraint run through his strong arms as he released her. While he went through into the bathroom she walked over to the window, pulling the long sweep of curtain aside a crack to stare out at the city lights and the eerie floodlit beauty of the Sacré-Coeur, pale against the night sky. Her heart was already racing from Glenn's touch, yet somehow she couldn't get into the large double bed and lie waiting for him to join her.

When he came out of the bathroom he was wearing a kneelength robe that showed his muscular legs and a glimpse of deeply tanned chest.

'I thought you'd be in bed,' he commented, with a smile that didn't temper the hunger she saw in his eyes. 'I always suspected you were a romantic.'

He came towards her and, taking her in his arms, he kissed her before carrying her to bed, sweeping back the sheets as he laid her down. With an economical movement he took off his robe and threw it aside, and she caught her breath at the power and grace of his naked male body. As he lowered himself to her, she was trembling.

'Please,' she whispered, as he started to take off her

nightgown. 'Please, Glenn, put the light off.'

'You don't have to be shy with me.'

'No, please,' she breathed, resisting him.

'Kira, I know you have scars,' he said, his voice a little ragged despite its gentleness. 'But you're still beautiful. I still want to look at you.'

But to calm her fears he reached out and switched off the lamp before his mouth found hers. A shudder shook her as, after a long, searching kiss, he went to slide her nightgown off her shoulders. She flinched and he murmured, his breath coming hard, 'Do you think a few scars make any difference to how incredibly beautiful you are? We were meant for each other. Always.'

'No,' she protested. 'That's not true. It was Stuart I loved.'

She wasn't prepared for the blaze of anger that came into his eyes. Then it faded and his hand stroked the line of her throat before his fingers brushed her breast.

'Forget you ever belonged to anyone else,' he breathed.

She was too tense to respond to him, but he was patient, caressing her lightly with his lips and hands while mutely she implored him to murmur not how she bewitched him, but that he loved her.

'Kira, what's the matter?' he asked, smoothing a strand of hair away from her face.

'I'm sorry,' she whispered. 'I . . . I just want to be left alone.'

'Left alone?' he repeated with harsh incredulity. 'You're my *wife*, Kira.'

'I may be,' she said, her voice rising, 'but tonight I don't want to make love.'

The line of his mouth went hard and his hands tightened on her shoulders.

'You've taxed my understanding to the limit. Now, you may not be in the mood, but I am.'

'It takes two for it to be any good. I would have

thought you knew that,' she said as she fought with him to let her get out of bed.

As her fist connected with his shoulder, Glenn swore, slamming hold of her wrists and pressing her back on the pillows. His eyes smouldering with anger, he snatched her nightgown from her and she heard the rip of the fine fabric.

'Maybe you don't find the gentle approach a turn-on,' he said gratingly, the weight of his hard man's body imprisoning her. 'In which case, let's try it this way.'

She could feel the heat of his body and his breath fanning her skin as frantically she tried to escape from the pressure of his thighs and chest.

'Let go of me,' she hissed.

'You're a wilful little cat and like all cats you think your soul's your own,' he said, his voice rough as, holding her protesting hands still, his mouth came down on hers. His kiss held no savagery, but it was far from gentle, making her feel plundered and invaded.

She struggled in desperation, horrified by the rage of hunger she sensed in him. He cupped a sure hand under her breast and, when finally his mouth left hers, she turned her head aside and sobbed, 'Glenn, please, not like this.'

He grabbed hold of her wrists, pinning them on either side of her face as he stared down on her.

'What the hell did you marry me for?' he demanded harshly. 'Now stop acting the puritan. You could scarcely wait for me to take you the last time.'

His angry intimate words made disgust swamp her. Fighting him with a woman's means, she bit his wrist in her struggle to free herself. Glenn gave a muttered curse and she kicked hard against his shins and succeeded in slithering away from him. Clutching at the sheet, she said, pale and livid, 'I married you for Heather. For Heather . . . do you understand? Because if you'd married Clare . . .'

She didn't get any further.

'You scheming little bitch!' he exploded in a voice resonant with fury. 'Well, you know the saying— you've made your bed and now you're damned well going to lie in it.'

'No!' she gasped as he ripped the sheet from her.

But her frantic cry was lost as his mouth came down on hers. His hard body pinioned her against the bed, while she struggled helplessly. She twisted her hips in a desperate attempt to escape from his nakedness. Aware of his arousal and terrified of his intention, she bit him again, lashing out wildly with her hands.

'Please,' she panted, scarcely able to find the breath to sob, 'don't do this to me!'

'Then stop fighting me,' he muttered thickly, his body heat searing her.

'And if not, you'll rape me?'

The fright and exhaustion in her voice, together with the ugly word, seemed to reach him. For an instant he held her rigid, his face so taut that only his eyes held a hard, steely light. Then abruptly, as though she repelled him, he released her, swinging his feet on to the carpet. He dragged a hand through his hair as he sat down on the side of the bed, before prowling in the darkness over to the window, savage anger in every line of his naked body.

With a faint sob Kira turned on her side, clenching a fistful of pillow, her throat thudding as she suppressed tears. Outside came the muted sound of a passing car, and then there was only the arid, menacing stillness. When finally she managed to speak, it was a tight, unhappy whisper.

'Why did you agree to marry me?'

He gave a harsh, mirthless laugh before saying with brutal sarcasm, 'As a rich widow with an enticing body, surely you can work it out. It's been my bad luck to have been short-changed on the sex.'

She bit her lip. If he had hit her she couldn't have felt greater pain. Her silent tears made the pillow damp beneath her cheek. Glenn could have had no idea she was crying bitterly till he heard her anguished sharply indrawn breath. A moment later she felt his hand on her shoulder, but she neither spoke nor moved to look at him. Instead she tensed, hating him with every nerve. The hand tightened as though with anger and then was withdrawn. A long while later she finally fell asleep.

When she woke it was morning and she was alone in the large bed. The aching pain of knowing what a sham her marriage was remained curiously untouched by the healing oblivion of sleep. Glenn was fastening his shirt and she watched with cold hostility the way the material played across his hard-muscled chest.

'So you're awake at last,' he began, his face tautly expressionless as he looked at her.

She pulled the sheet protectively about her as she sat up.

'Will you pass me my wrap?' she asked, staggered that her voice could sound so coldly even.

Glenn came towards her and sat down on the bed. He took hold of her wrist, examining the bracelet of faint bruises that showed on her fair skin.

'We got off to a good start last night, didn't we?' he said in a harsh undertone.

'What did you expect?' she said, her eyes full of animosity.

'What I expected,' he said, throwing the sarcastic words at her, 'was a wife who'd show a little warmth and affection in bed.'

'That, as well as my money?' she said with a tight little laugh. She looked down so he wouldn't see how close to tears she was, and said in a low resentful voice, 'You were an absolute brute to me last night.'

Glenn caught hold of her by the shoulders.

'It didn't have to be like that!'

'No,' she agreed bitterly. 'I'm your wife and that means I have to allow you your marital rights, so I suppose it's my fault if you decide to rape me.'

'You got what you deserved,' he said harshly, checking his temper as he added stonily, 'But don't worry. There won't be a repeat performance.'

'No, you're right, there won't. Because I won't be fool enough to fight you the next time. After all, as your *wife*, I don't have the right to short-change you where sex is concerned. But after this, don't expect from me what I gave Stuart. He loved me, and he'd never have bruised me and hurt me the way you did last night.'

She saw his eyes harden and knew with a fierce sense of redress that she had succeeded in repaying him for the cruel words he had said to her. Yet it gave no ease to the desolation that tore at her heart.

The honeymoon was a disaster. The sultry heat of Paris and the beauty of the Seine, with its many famous landmarks that would normally have captivated her, left her unmoved. The bruises on her wrists soon faded, but the emotional devastation of his callous words remained. How right she had been not to let herself love him. To cover how desperately unhappy she was, all through the weekend she was distant and accusing with him, killing any chance to even start to put things right.

They flew into Heathrow late on Sunday. Kira's spirits lifted temporarily as she saw Heather waving excitedly to her, and she was glad she had thought to slip the bottle of Miss Dior she had bought for her into her bag.

She hugged Heather and kissed Beth while Glenn exchanged a few words with Beth's husband, Jon.

'Was Paris as magical as ever?' Beth smiled.

'Yes, it was lovely,' Kira lied, conscious of Glenn's

icy blue eyes on her.

'Well, Heather's all ready for Canada tomorrow,' Beth said. 'And she's been no trouble.'

Kira squeezed her stepdaughter's hand. It felt good to be home. Home! The word suddenly struck. Home wasn't the stately Edwardian house she had shared with Stuart. Home was Glenn's place, a place in which she would never feel now she belonged.

In the back seat of the Mercedes Heather talked animatedly. Kira was glad of her happy chatter, of anything which dispelled the menacing tension between her and Glenn. As he opened the car door for her, Heather scrambled out of the back.

'Are you going to carry Kira over the threshhold, Uncle Glenn?' she asked.

'They only do that in films, Heather,' Kira said quickly.

She saw Glenn stab her a glance and sensed that the antagonism was slowly building up to some kind of flash point.

'You must get to bed, pet,' she went on hurriedly. 'It's late and we're all tired. And tomorrow's going to be a very busy day.'

She took the little girl up to her room and saw her into bed. Heather, who was excited both about flying out to Canada and her new bedroom, wasn't the least bit sleepy, and Kira sat with her for a while, conscious of how much she was going to miss her.

She kissed her goodnight and then went out on to the landing, hesitating indecisively. Then swiftly she went into one of the spare rooms and locked the door. Some time she and Glen would have to resolve the problems in their marriage. He hadn't touched her since their wedding night, but presumably now that they were home he'd expect to make love to her. Although she'd told him she'd acquiesce to his demands, that wasn't how she felt tonight. She knew she'd resist him and she didn't want a fraught, bitter atmosphere in the house before Heather left for Canada tomorrow morning. By sleeping alone the discord between her and Glenn would remain smouldering but still subdued.

It was only after she had watched the Air Canada plane lift off from the tarmac the next day that she realised that she and her husband were alone to sort things out. He had teased Heather affectionately over breakfast, but with Kira he had been derisively polite. Some sort of frightening flare-up between them seemed inevitable.

During dinner that evening she was deliberately remote with him. The best she could hope for now in their marriage was a practical arrangement where she acted as a housekeeper and hostess for him and kept him satisfied in bed. The rage and pain of her disillusionment made her want to nettle him, heedless of the danger of provoking him too far with her icy reserve.

She suggested they take their coffee into the drawing-room and he agreed with equal politeness, though his jawline was set hard. He sat down on the sofa while she walked across the room to an armchair.

'No, come over here,' he said, and she heard the steel in his voice beneath the softness.

Her heart had started thudding. Avoiding his gaze she set her cup down on the coffee-table and said casually, 'I'm comfortable here.'

'I said, come here.'

Rebellion flashed in her eyes. Defensively she got to her feet. The silence in the room seemed suddenly dense and incalculable. She was about to escape quickly, but Glenn got to his feet with lightning reflexes and snatched hold of her.

'Let go of me,' she hissed.

He tilted her chin up with angry fingers. Conscious of his nearness and his lean, virile strength, she felt vulnerable and shatteringly aware of the unresolved sexual unrest between them.

'I thought you'd agreed that you'd let me have my marital rights, as you so quaintly call them,' Glenn mocked with harsh derision.

'I did,' she said, pulling away.

'Then what was the spare room episode about last night?' he asked gratingly.

'You know damned well what it was about,' she flared. 'I don't want to sleep with you.'

'But if I insist you'll sacrifice yourself. Is that what you're saying?' he demanded with savage sarcasm.

'Yes, if you want to put it like that,' she answered, her eyes warring with his, despite the fact that she was having to clench her hands to stop them trembling.

Glenn pulled her angrily towards him, his fingers biting into her arms.

'Tell me, does acting frigid give you some kind of buzz?' he asked.

'*Rape* doesn't give me a buzz,' she retaliated, her voice taut and within a notch of breaking.

He released her so suddenly that she staggered. She clutched at the back of the armchair as he said tersely, 'And sleeping with Stuart's ghost in the bed isn't much of a turn on, either.'

He left the room while Kira sank down in the armchair, covering her face with her hands.

In the days that followed she felt she was living out a charade of normality. She went to work, behaved with the same cheerfulness and care towards her patients, knowing all the time that her marriage was disintegrating. The atmosphere in the house seemed so taut that Kira couldn't understand how she and Glenn somehow kept it from snapping. When he informed her that he would be leaving first thing on Saturday morning to drive to his accounting institute's headquarters just below Marlow, on the Thames, to lecture on an accountancy workshop, he was curt and detached. Kira received the news with relief. She needed time to do some thinking.

Glenn didn't comment again on the fact that she was still sleeping in a separate room. Only when she met him on the landing, wearing only her nightgown, having finished her beauty routine in the bathroom, did he remark sarcastically, 'You don't have to run away from me, Kira, I'm not going to force myself on you.'

She gave him a look of silent hostility and went hurriedly past him into her room. She sat down on the bed, wondering how they could ever begin to bridge the gulf of antagonism that now separated them.

For a long time she lay awake, very conscious that he was just across the landing from her. How was it possible that when she knew there was no bond of love between them, part of her still needed to be physically close with him? If she went to him, couldn't she hope to make him love her, if only a little? Impatiently she put the notion out of her mind, yet her need for him remained.

When she finally slept it was to dream again of the car crash in which Stuart had been killed. Fantasy blended curiously with fact in a vivid nightmare world that had her running down a stark hospital corridor, desperately searching for Stuart, while the hopeless fear pressed in on her that he was already dead. Ahead of her a hospital orderly came out of a room, wheeling a white-sheeted body. She screamed, struggling to reach out to Stuart, to stop him from being taken away, but something was holding her back.

'Kira, it's all right. It's only a nightmare. You're safe.'

The intense voice shattered the torment of her dream, and she awoke to find she was safe in Glenn's arms. With a muffled sob she turned her wet face into his shoulder, finding comfort in the live warmth of his strong male body. But even in the haven of his close pressing arms the trauma of the nightmare persisted for a moment or two.

'I killed him,' she moaned softly. '*I* was driving. *I* killed him.'

Glenn let her sob out the whole torment of the nightmare, his hands stroking her back while she clung to him tightly. She could feel the steady beat of his heart as he held her close, and she rubbed her cheek against his solid chest, deriving pleasure and reassurance from its hairy roughness. As she quietened Glenn asked, his hand smoothing her hair, 'Is this the first time you've had a nightmare like this?'

'No,' she whispered. 'Ever since the crash.'

'You've got to stop blaming yourself,' he insisted. 'It wasn't your fault.'

'Yes, it was,' she whispered miserably. 'You just don't know. I was so stubborn. I had to make an argument over who should drive that day.' Tears came into her eyes again as she added, her voice catching, 'It was all my fault. I never made him happy.'

Glenn grabbed hold of her by the shoulders and she gave a gasp of surprise at his unexpected explosion of anger.

'For God's sake, will you stop it?' he said, raising his voice to her as he had never done before. 'Stuart didn't deserve your love, let alone the way you're tormenting yourself.'

'What do you mean?' she demanded heatedly.

'I mean, you blind little fool, he was cheating on you in the whole of the last year of your marriage.'

There was a sudden appalled silence and then Glenn swore savagely and harshly. He stood up from the bed and strode out of the room.

CHAPTER TEN

THE SOUND of the slammed door faded, leaving a shocked, gaping stillness. Kira switched on the light and then sat hugging her arms, her mind racing with what Glenn had told her in anger. After the initial shock, fury had taken over. How dare Glenn come out with such a contemptible lie? She wanted to make him take it back, to hear him admit that he had said it just to hurt her.

And all the time beneath the outrage there was the reluctant, dazed comprehension that what Glenn had told her wasn't a lie at all. She tried to resist it with angry resentment, but anger couldn't erode the implacable truth. This explained so much that before she hadn't understood and had wanted to deny. This was why she had sensed something was wrong between her and Stuart. She'd thought the spontaneity had gone out of their lovemaking because Stuart had been reluctant to try for a baby. A knife of pain stabbed at her heart as she realised the real reason why they'd stopped being so close physically was that he had a mistress. How could she not have guessed?

She stood up and pulled on her wrap. She couldn't sleep now and she didn't want to lie awake thinking of Stuart's unfaithfulness in the long hours before morning.

She went downstairs and into the kitchen and mechanically filled the kettle and set it on the gas. Her first emotional reaction to the truth was spent, leaving her with a numbed sense of realism that no longer flinched from what Glenn had told her. She wondered with a slight sense of surprise why she didn't feel more devastated. Was the reason shock?

The kettle boiled and as she was pouring the water into the teapot Glenn came into the kitchen. He spoke immediately, running a strong, tanned hand through his dark hair as he began, 'Kira, you have to forget what I said to you just now. It's not true. I only said it because I'd had enough of watching you torment your-self over an accident you couldn't possibly have prevented. I wanted to jolt you out of it, but I chose a damned stupid way to go about it. I'm sorry.'

She looked at him, noting the directness with which his eyes met hers and their hawkish keenness. His manner and his words were convincing. Perhaps that was the problem. They were too convincing.

'You don't have to lie to me, Glenn,' she said quietly, trying to keep her voice steady. 'I've thought it through and it makes sense.'

He took hold of her forcefully by the shoulders.

'No, it doesn't,' he said vehemently. 'You're not thinking straight. Forget what I said.'

'I can't.' She caught her breath. 'Tell me . . . tell me, was Stuart really on his way to a business conference in Jersey when we were in that smash-up, or was he . . .?' She hesitated. Even to say it hurt. 'Or was he going to be with . . . with the woman he was having an affair with?'

'I've told you,' Glenn said. 'He didn't have a mistress.'

Kira didn't contradict him. Yet despite his force-fulness and his apparent sincerity she knew he was lying to her now. Glenn pulled her to him, holding her against him while he brushed her temple with his lips.

'Christ knows what possessed me to tell you that lie,' he said almost angrily before he released her and moved to the worktop to pour some brandy into her tea. 'Take it up to bed,' he said, handing her the cup. 'It will help you sleep.'

She didn't argue. She needed to be on her own to make some sense out of her feelings. It wasn't just reaction to what Glenn had told her about Stuart that had left her so confused. She knew he was trying to protect her, and the knowledge stirred some faint memory that refused to come into focus.

She went back to bed and sipped the hot tea thoughtfully. Slowly the flaw in her marriage to Stuart became clearer. She had been right in what she had suspected. He hadn't loved her. The truth flashed into stark prominence. She wasn't thinking just of the fact that he had been unfaithful to her. She was thinking how, immediately after the accident, when his own life hadn't seemed to be in danger, he'd made Glenn Heather's guardian. It wasn't the action of a man tormented by uncertainty as to whether his wife was going to pull through. And yet she'd always had the shadowy impression that somehow he'd been with her through the insubstantial hours while she fought to maintain her hold on life. She gave the problem up. Perhaps, although it had taken time to contact him, her father had sat with her. It couldn't have been Stuart.

Not till she was drifting off into an emotionally exhausted sleep did the realisation come. It had been Glenn whose presence she had sensed beside her in the hospital room, willing her to survive.

When she woke, the sunlight was bright behind the curtains. She glanced quickly at the bedside clock and saw that it was after nine. Filled with a sense of urgency, she ran hurriedly downstairs, compelled by the thought that she must see Glenn before he left for the accountancy workshop.

She ran into the kitchen and then stopped dead. From out of the window she could see his car was no longer in the drive. He had left without saying goodbye, and as she looked round the kitchen she saw

that he had not even left a note. Disappointed,
suddenly she remembered why she had been so
desperate to see him before he left. She had wanted to
tell him how overwhelmingly she loved him.

She could admit it now. Only a man who cared for
her deeply could have sat by her bedside while she
fought for life. She had been so careful for so long to
hide the true nature of her feelings from herself in her
fear of being hurt by rejection, that she wasn't sure
when she had first fallen in love with Glenn. Perhaps it
dated back as far as her return from Provence when
there had been that sudden mellowing in their
relationship.

With a stir of deep contrition she thought of how
hatefully cold she had been with him. Now all she
wanted was to put things right, to tell him that what
had happened on their wedding night had been more
her fault than his. Because he'd only ever said he'd
wanted her, she'd refused to acknowledge that she
loved him and that Heather had only been one of the
reasons why she'd married him.

The telephone interrupted her thoughts and she went
to answer it, her heart giving a leap of expectation that it
might be Glenn. Instead it was the estate agent. Clients
who had viewed her old house the previous week
wanted to look over it again, and the agent thought
they were very likely to put in an offer. As Kira wanted
to collect a few more things, she said she'd be there at
ten-thirty to show them around.

The couple hadn't arrived when she got there, and
she wandered aimlessly through the rooms, thinking of
the years she had spent there with Stuart. It was
strange, but although she'd loved him she felt no
jealousy of his mistress, and even her initial hurt and
anger had faded to a musing sadness.

Stuart had always needed acquisitions to make him
feel good. He'd wanted a prestigious house, a sleek,

expensive car. Presumably he'd seen a woman in those terms, too. She'd been a useful accessory in his life-style, a wife thirteen years younger than himself, whom he could show off to his friends. Once the newness had tarnished on their marriage he'd needed an affair, another woman to impress.

For the first time she could look back on her marriage without feeling guilty that she had pressurised him over wanting a baby. It hadn't been her fault that tensions had developed in their marriage. The accident hadn't been her fault either. She could accept it now as one of those tragedies that happened. She was finally free from the past, able to look back without pain and self-recrimination.

The doorbell rang and she went to let the clients in. She had no regrets now about selling the house. It wasn't home any more. The future belonged to her and Glenn.

She wished he wasn't going to be away till mid-week. It was hard to grasp, when he had always been so brutally cold with her when Stuart was alive, that in fact he'd cared about her, perhaps even loved her. Her heart jolted with the thought. Was it possible that Glenn had always loved her, that the derisive polite-ness had been a smoke-screen so effective she had misread it for hate? It scarcely seemed possible, yet it would be in character with a man who was always utterly self-contained.

Now, more than ever, she knew she had to talk to him and be honest about her feelings. With new strength and conviction she was certain she could save their marriage. She had decided to phone him when a better idea occurred to her. Tomorrow was Sunday. She'd drive to the institute's headquarters and they could have lunch together.

The headquarters was an old Victorian residence that had been added to with an impressive series of modern extensions. Its grounds sloped down to the Thames and the whole scene was overlaid with a rural Sunday tranquillity. The lavish sunlight increased her optimism. She was going to put everything right.

She found a parking space close to the porticoed entrance and went inside to ask at the desk for Glenn's room number. The lift carried her swiftly up to the third floor and she hurried along the thickly carpeted corridor.

The door to Glenn's room was ajar and she could see in quite clearly, glimpsing an expanse of pale beige carpet and a truncated view of the double bed. Hearing voices, she slowed her pace, and then she stopped, emotion bringing a surge of colour to her face as she leant weakly against the wall. Clare was sitting on the bed, held tightly in Glenn's arms.

She heard him say in a tender voice he had never used with her, 'No, I can't tell you I'll forget last night, any more than you will, but . . .'

Kira didn't stop to hear the rest. She started to run back along the corridor. A girl pushing a huge trolley laden with towels and bedlinen moved aside and stood staring after her. Kira didn't care. Nothing mattered except getting out of the building. The lift was already at the third floor and mercifully empty when the doors slid open.

She stepped inside, pressed the button for the ground floor and then leant shakily against the side of the lift, brushing a hand against the hot tear that ran down her cheek. Emotion tore at her. The irony that she should discover Glenn had slept with Clare so soon after learning that Stuart had been unfaithful to her stabbed like a knife.

There were a number of people standing chatting in the reception area and, knowing she couldn't cross it when she was so obviously crying, she went swiftly into the ladies' rest-room. She took a tissue from the box behind the washbasin and pressed it to her eyes, seeing as she looked up her dazed reflection in the mirror. She gave a muffled sob as she struggled to master angry tears. Had she driven Glenn to this because she'd been so cold with him, or had Clare been in the background ever since their marriage, making absurd all her thoughts and hopes?

From out of memory Glenn's voice mocked her. 'You're a rich widow with a house worth close on three hundred thousand pounds, before we even consider your other assets.' She'd persuaded herself yesterday that when he'd said on their wedding night he'd married her for money and for scx he'd been getting back at her, that they'd been angry words he hadn't meant. But now she was tormented by renewed uncertainy; Glenn had told her money was the reason Nigel had been interested in her, but did it apply equally to himself?

The cloakroom door opened and two women came in, chatting. Hurriedly Kira turned from the washbasin and walked past them. She didn't want anyone to see how upset she was. She wanted to get away, to be by herself where the pain she felt wouldn't be exacerbated by the need to present a calm outward front.

She crossed the reception area briskly, knowing that she must fight back the tears or she'd start to cry uncontrollably. Ahead of her, through the swing doors, she could see the sunlit car park, the massive blue cedar that lent serenity to the grounds. Everything was the same as when a few minutes ago she had entered the building. Its tranquillity mocked her.

'Kira?' There was surprise in Glenn's voice.

She started as she heard him call out to her. In a panic she pushed through the swing doors as though she hadn't heard him, quickening her steps to a run as she headed for her new car. She reached it, knowing he was following her, and somehow she managed to pull herself together as he came up to her.

The bright sunlight accentuated the saturnine lines of his face. She was conscious of his advantage over her in height and of the way his pristine shirt emphasised his attractive swarthiness. Her throat tightened and, with a supreme effort, she fought against a sharp uprise of emotion. If she thought of Clare she would break down.

Glenn put a casual hand on her shoulder as he bent to kiss her. She stiffened, as though his touch repelled her, and the warmth went out of his eyes.

'Hello, Kira,' he began evenly. 'What brings you here this morning? I couldn't believe it when I saw you in the foyer?'

Her words came suddenly. She didn't have to think of them. They were like a reflex action.

'I'm leaving you,' she said in a voice bitter with antagonism. 'I've had enough. I shan't be there when you get back.'

'What the hell are you talking about?'

'You heard me,' she said, infusing her voice with cold hatred because that was the only way she could keep it steady. 'Our marriage is over.'

He grabbed hold of her by the arm.

'Now listen, if this is because of what I said to you the other night,' he began harshly, 'I've already told you I'm sorry about it.'

'And you *dared* to tell me Stuart was unfaithful to me,' she said venomously. 'My God, when I think about it . . .'

She broke off, unable to continue.

'You're taxing my patience to the limit, Kira,' Glenn said tersely. 'Stuart is dead and I've respected your feelings for him long enough.'

'I hate you,' she said as she snatched her arm free. 'I don't know why you ever married me.'

'I'm beginning to wonder myself,' he replied with

exasperated anger.

'Then undoubtedly you'll be very relieved to know I'm leaving.'

For a crazy instant she hoped he'd explode into possessive male fury and tell her she wasn't going anywhere. But instead he said, his voice clipped and cold, though his jaw was a tight, uncompromising line, 'I suppose you intend moving back into your old house. OK. Maybe it's not such a bad idea.'

She didn't answer him. She swept him a look of hatred and then turned and unlocked the car door. Without glancing at him she started the engine and pulled away. Only as she was going down the drive did she look in the rear mirror to see him walking back into the building, his pace quickening so that it held all of its usual leashed energy. She felt the tightness in her throat would strangle her and realised that when she had told him she was walking out on him she had never expected him to let her go so easily. She felt betrayed and humiliated and chilled with a desolation that went beyond tears.

By the time she got home her mood had changed. She didn't stop to consider what had happened to the calm, thoughtful woman who had accepted and forgiven Stuart's infidelity. She was consumed by a towering rage against Glenn that made her wish furiously that instead of the cold confrontation she had had with him she had struck him and told him she'd seen him with Clare. And then the anger abated a little and she started to go over the short time they'd been married, knowing that she should never have been so distant with him, and that if she hadn't possibly this wouldn't have happened.

She'd caused the rift in their marriage to widen, but she knew suddenly that she wasn't stepping quietly out of the way while she lost Glenn to Clare. She was going to fight to keep her marriage alive, and that meant she wasn't walking out, however hard it was to swallow her damaged pride and stay.

Over the next three days she was glad of work which meant that for odd moments when she was at the hospital Glenn faded from her thoughts. The rest of the time was a kind of torture when she assumed he was with Clare, in her company at best while at worst, in her bed.

Had he turned to Clare because she'd almost driven him to it, or did he find Clare more attractive? By the time she heard his key turn in the front door late on Wednesday evening her nerves and her temper were stretched tight.

He came into the lounge where she was watching the end of the ten o'clock news. The newscaster's voice read on into a silence that had become tense and charged with undercurrents. Kira reached for the remote control switch that was in front of her on the coffee-table, conscious that her hand was trembling.

As she switched the set to standby, Glenn advanced into the room and said, his resolute voice ominously even, 'I didn't expect to find you here. Did you forget something?'

The edge of sarcasm was barely detectable, but she caught it instantly and got swiftly to her feet.

'That's the sort of cheap remark I'd expect from you!'

'What are you doing here?' he asked. 'I thought I'd find you at Stuart's, but your things aren't there. Just what are you playing at, Kira?'

'It's what *you're* playing at that I'd like to know. Did you call in at the other house to make sure the coast was clear here?' she asked with defensive cold haughtiness.

'I don't follow your last cryptic comment,' Glenn said derisively. 'But yes, I did call in at Stuart's.'

'Why?' she demanded.

He shrugged his jacket off angrily and threw it on to a chair, not answering immediately. The taut silence lengthened. Kira hesitated and then realised suddenly she couldn't brace herself to ask outright if he wanted her to stay. Instead she said in a rather cool voice, 'Do you want a drink?'

He caught hold of her arm as she went towards the drinks cabinet, his grip so savage it made her gasp.

'No, damn you. I want to know what this is all about.'

She thought of him with Clare and in that instant all her hot, pent-up fury came to the surface and she swung her hand up and slapped him with resounding force. Glenn swore, his eyes glinting with anger.

'That is the last time you ever slap my face,' he said menacingly. 'Do you understand?'

'You deserved it,' she retaliated. 'You deserved it and more. I don't know whatever made me think I'd give our marriage another try . . .'

'My God, you mean . . . Is that why you're still here?' he demanded, comprehension coming and stripping the anger from his voice as he cut across her.

'Yes,' she confessed mutinously, her eyes warring with his.

'What is this?' he asked with slow suspicion. 'Your way of stretching the rack a little? You want to go on sleeping in another room, slapping my face every time I touch you, making me feel guilty of rape because I know that's the only way you'll ever let me have you?'

'That's never been what I've wanted,' she denied heatedly. 'What I want is for our marriage to work.'

His narrowed eyes stabbed hers, and conscious that her heart was starting to race a little, she dropped her gaze and asked in a constrained voice that was not quite steady, 'Do you want me to stay, Glenn?'

He tilted her chin up, forcing her gaze to meet his. She felt a slight tremor run through his hand that gripped her arm and she sensed, without understanding it, that she was pushing him to the limit of his temper.

'To go on with the same charade of you sleeping in a separate room?' he mocked.

She remembered Clare and her eyes went hot and stormy.

'No,' she said angrily, resisting the wild impulse to hit out at him again.

'The willing victim?' His short laugh was harsh and with it her self-control snapped and she raised her hand.

Glenn snatched hold of it and, as he did so, suddenly she couldn't stop trembling. His merciless eyes searched her face and then, inexplicably, the hardness went out of them. He drew her into his arms, holding her closely for a long time while she pressed tightly to him. She had abandoned thought. She only knew how much she loved him, how desperately she needed him.

'Love me,' she whispered shakenly, curling her fingers in the hair at the nape of his neck. 'I want you, Glenn. I want you so much.'

He looked down at her, his voice strangely intense as he demanded, 'Tell me again. Swear to me you're not walking out.'

'Never,' she whispered. 'But love me. Please love me.'

'You don't have to ask, Kira,' he said raggedly,.

He cupped his hand behind her neck, his lips almost bruising as he kissed her with a deep, raw passion. She answered him hungrily, her body on fire with a longing that was as fierce as her desire to forget he had ever been unfaithful to her. She could sense the violent passion in the way he held her, but it didn't frighten her. Instead she exulted in it, her lips answering his as though with the longing of years.

When at last he raised his head her breathing was quick and ragged. Glenn gave a groan of satisfaction, his eyes watching the colour that flared in her face before he combed his hands into her hair and kissed her again, this time his mouth more gentle as his lips parted hers. She tilted her head back as his mouth left hers to travel down her throat.

'Make me forget,' she pleaded urgently, knowing that unless the memory of Clare was obliterated it would be agony to respond to him fully. 'Make me drown in forgetfulness.'

'Just let go, Kira. Don't hold back with me this time,' he breathed.

His hands caressed her back, drawing her more tightly against him, and with a race of pleasure and anticipation she felt his need of her. His mouth found hers again, its sensual demand making her body come alive with a driving desire. She felt his hand slip possessively to cup her breast and she broke the kiss with a gasp of bewildered pleasure, her eyes, dark and feverish, meeting the blaze of passion in his, as murmuring his name she slipped impatient hands inside his shirt. She traced her fingers over the wiry hairs of his broad chest, feeling a shudder rack him.

'God, you're a mystery to me,' Glenn breathed harshly as he swept her into his arms, his mouth claiming hers as he carried her up to the double room she had never shared with him.

He lowered her on to the bed, his eyes holding hers as he started to unfasten her blouse. She turned her head on the pillow, giving herself up to the mindless pleasure of his knowing hands. Then his lips brushed her breasts, arousing her to a trembling need that made her crave to feel his body a part of hers. By the time he had undressed her his hands had learned every inch of her, trapping her in a dark vortex of feverish desire. She moaned softly as she felt his naked body the length of hers, any notion she might have had of holding some part of herself back from him shattering as she gave in to her need to explore all of his male body with urgent fingers.

She had the fleeting, instinctive comprehension that he intended that she should lose herself to him completely, and in the urgency of her need for him nothing mattered save that the dazzling, frenzied pleasure should shatter in the explosion of climax. She cried out as his mouth teased her taut nipples to peaks of arousal, thrusting her hips up to his as the pitch of pleasure tightened unbearably. Her fingers dug into his strong back, her legs encircling him as he possessed her. And then the emotional reaction to perfect unity with him was too much and she burst into violent sobs.

Glenn gathered her to him as she fell into cataclysmic freedom. His body after his complete possession of her was warm and protective as he held her close. She cried helplessly, feeling the brush of his lips against her tumbled hair.

'It's all right,' he said gently. He drew a deep breath and then murmured, 'Kira, you were wonderful.'

'Tell me you love me,' she whispered, still shaken with crying and the complete abandonment with which she had given herself to him that was outside anything she had ever known before. 'I don't care if it's not true. Just tell me so that tonight I can believe it.

He shifted so that he could look down at her, his blue eyes probing hers. Her vision was misted with tears and, in the darkness, she couldn't interpret what she saw in his gaze. For an instant it almost seemed like angry puzzlement and then it faded and his hand smoothed her disordered hair before he drew her against him so that her cheek rested against his chest.

'You'll never know what a delight and a torment you are to me,' he said, the quietness of his voice seeming to italicise its sincerity. 'Of course I love you. You're everything to me.'

His hands were gentle on the curve of her hips, and she stirred a little and pressed a kiss against the strong column of his throat. She couldn't doubt the sincerity of his words. What had happened between him and Clare didn't matter any more.

She lay in his embrace, enfolded by the after-bliss of their lovemaking. Overwhelmed by the intensity of response he had drawn her to, she felt lulled and complete. She could sense the peacefulness in Glenn's powerful body as she lay curled against him, not talking nor stirring, while the beauty of feeling made seconds seem an eternity in the moments before she slipped into sleep.

When she woke, a sensuous languor made her stretch out lazily and she opened her eyes to see Glenn, one arm resting on the pillow as he watched her face. The memory of his lovemaking made her reach out a hand to trace her fingers tenderly over the warm strength of his chest. He took her hand in his, raising the palm slowly to his lips. His blue eyes held hers for a long moment before he said, his voice quiet and resolute, 'I love you.'

She smiled softly at him, emotion catching at her throat as she whispered, 'I know.'

She slipped her hand out of his so she could slide it caressingly along the strong line of his jaw, her movements making the covers slip to reveal the swell of her breasts. Glenn kissed her mouth gently and then brushed her temple with his lips as he drew her into his arms so that she lay with her head against his shoulder.

'What time do you have to be at work this morning?' she asked dreamily.

'I thought I'd get into the office about ten,' he said, and she heard the humour in his voice.

She glanced up, her eyes laughing as they met his, and then they faltered and became confused as Clare flashed into her mind.

'What is it?' Glenn asked quietly.

She shook her head.

'Nothing,' she lied quickly, quelling the thought. She would let nothing spoil their magical unity.

She felt his hand stroke her waist and gave a sigh of pleasure. This time his lovemaking was a slow delight, different completely from the fierce passion of the night before. She had fought her feelings for him for so long that it was only now that she was learning the range of his loving.

He took her to a higher and higher plane of pleasure until the explosive release of climax gave her the tempestuous joy of feeling the rhythm kisses her body was helplessly bestowing on him, as with him inside her she embraced him over and over again, her body pulsating and glorying in the depth of his penetration, in the ecstasy of love she was bestowing and receiving.

Later, when her heartbeat had steadied and the blossoming of her body had left her totally at peace, she stirred and reached for Glenn's hand.

'I never knew it could be so beautiful,' she murmured, 'that I could feel this way.'

Glenn moved so that he could feel her soft warmth against him. He trailed a caressing finger down her cheek.

'You're a very sensual woman,' he said softly. 'You need to love and you need to be loved.'

'I needed you to love me last night,' she admitted with a contented sigh.

'And this morning?' Glenn joked, his eyes gently teasing as they held hers. 'I didn't detect any reluctance, or are my antennae not working well?'

'Everything about you is working well,' she laughed, colouring slightly and putting his strong male hand to her lips to kiss it.

CHAPTER ELEVEN

EVERYTHING should have been perfect. Instead it just missed by a narrow and almost imperceptible margin. Heather had phoned from Canada and was obviously, from her breathless excitement, having a wonderful time. Work was going well. In fact, after months of painstaking treatment that had seemed to produce no tangible results, one of the handicapped patients made a marked breakthrough in progress, delighting everyone in the medical team. Kira's first entertaining as Glenn's wife was an unqualified success, and, having always been very relationless, she appreciated the way his family drew her into their circle.

Yet some elusive element was missing, though she tried hard to deny it. With the physical side of her relationship with Glenn strong, she was discovering other shared pleasures of being close with him. Their sense of communication was something stimulating and exciting. At times the vibrations of pairing between them were so strong, she couldn't believe anything could ever threaten her marriage. Glenn's sense of humour and forceful personality seemed to satisfy every need in her nature, while his varied, uninhibited lovemaking sparked in her a feverish, unstinting response.

It was afterwards that sobs would shake her, sobs she couldn't seem to check and that his protectiveness couldn't abate. When finally he demanded, almost roughly, what was wrong, she shook her head and couldn't answer. He knew her emotions ran deep and he let it go at that. She was glad he didn't question her.

She couldn't bring herself to talk to him about Clare. She wanted to forget her.

But it wasn't easy. When he didn't come home from work at the usual time one evening she couldn't help but remember the times Stuart had come in, complaining wearily he'd been held up at the office. Naïvely she'd believed him. It had never crossed her mind to suspect he was having an affair. But she wasn't naïve any longer, and furthermore she knew Glenn had slept with Clare before. Was there something wrong with her that meant that neither of the men she had married could be faithful to her? As the clock went slowly round, she worked herself up into a fever of suspicion.

It had been an oppressive day, laden with the heat of high summer, and now there was the uneasy roll of thunder in the distance, adding to the atmosphere of waiting. When at last she heard Glenn's car turn into the drive she was tense with accusations she knew she wouldn't make.

'Hello, sweetheart,' he said as he came into the lounge. 'I'm sorry I'm so late. I got held up in a meeting that went on and on. It's a wonder we got any agreement at all with so many trenchant opinions.'

It would have been easier to have believed him if he had seemed tired and a trace irritable. Instead he seemed full of pithy energy. Had the meeting, with its challenge of getting an agreement, stimulated him, or was it a woman's company? She clamped down on the thought.

'It doesn't matter,' she said a shade stiffly. 'I thought we'd have something cold tonight anyway, so there's no problem with dinner.'

'Fine,' he said. 'Or if you like we could go out for a meal?'

'No, I'd rather stay in,' she answered.

She saw his eyes narrow a little on her face and felt

the old prickle of anticipation that they were building up to some kind of confrontation. Almost impatiently she got up and went into the kitchen. She didn't expect there to be anything placid and quiet about their relationship to confirm its strength. The sexual magnetism between them created too much static for that. What was lacking in their relationship was trust.

Glenn followed her into the kitchen as she was tossing the salad.

'So who was at the meeting?' she asked with careful indifference, not turning from the worktop.

'You don't want me to bore you with the details, do you?' Glenn answered casually.

What she wanted was for him to confirm that he had actually spent the evening at work. Her already taut nerves tightened.

'Not if you don't want to tell me,' she said with a trace of coolness.

He took hold of her by the shoulders and turned her to face him, his astute blue eyes probing hers. Her gaze warred with his and he gave a low sound in his throat before cupping his hand behind her neck and kissing her possessively and with sensual demand. Her mind clamoured and rebelled, while her body betrayed her with a kindling of hot-blooded pleasure.

As though he sensed her resistance, he drew her against him more intimately and, as he did so, a sudden vertigo enveloped her. In dizzy alarm she put a protesting hand against his chest and gave a faint moan. Instantly he raised his mouth from hers, holding her while she swayed against him. She couldn't see his face clearly and her heart was thudding sickeningly, increasing the roaring in her head.

'Kira, what is it?' he demanded, his voice roughened with concern.

'I think I'm going to faint,' she whispered, engulfed by a sickening weakness. The light seemed to be receding and a trembling iciness was spreading over her.

When she came to a few minutes later she was lying on the sofa in the lounge. Glenn was saying her name and she managed to say, not very convincingly, 'I'm all right.'

His eyes were intent on her face as he held her hand in his warm grasp, his thumb moving in a caress over her fingers.

'Lie still,' he ordered quietly as, shakily, she tried to sit up.

Emotion tightened her throat and she closed her eyes so he wouldn't see the pain and uncertainty in them. How could he be so protective with her if he was involved with Clare? And yet she knew he had slept with her once. What did Clare offer him that she was unable to satisfy?

'I'll get you a drink of cold water,' he said, feathering a caress across her cheek. 'It's the heat that's made you faint. It's very airless tonight.'

He came back with a tumbler of iced water and put it into her hand. For an instant, her eyes, filled with questioning, met his. He drew his brows together, accentuating the shrewdness of his swarthy face.

'What is it?' he asked a shade curtly. 'Why are you looking at me like that?'

'I'm not,' she denied hurriedly. 'I don't know what you mean.'

A fleeting expression almost of anger crossed his face and he stood up, his body taut and powerful as he paced a short distance away from her, before turning back to say, his voice resolute and even, 'I've been thinking. Could you arrange to take the next fortnight off work?'

'Yes, with a bit of skilful negotiating I should think so,' she said. 'Why?'

'I'd like us to take a holiday. Our honeymoon wasn't

what it should have been. We need some time together, Kira.'

So he'd sensed things still weren't completely right between them. Yet how could they be when Clare was in the background? Yes, she had been cold with him, but how quickly he'd turned to Clare when their marriage had been under intense pressure. She rubbed a tired hand briefly across her forehead, wishing she could find the answers she needed. Did Glenn love her, or did he only want her physically? Was the emotional rapport she sensed between them illusory?

'I'd like a holiday,' she agreed, summoning up a faint smile.

Glenn insisted she get an early night, which seemed a good idea. When she woke the next morning she could hear it raining heavily, the tree outside the bedroom window dripping steadily.

Glenn was dressing.

'How are you feeling?' he asked.

She smiled at him, remembering how caring and tender he had been last night. He had cradled her in his arms, his words as soothing as his even breathing, until somewhere in the quiet conversation she had fallen asleep, enveloped by his protectiveness.

'I feel much better,' she told him. 'I'll get up and make breakfast.'

'No, have a lie-in,' he said. 'I'm not stopping for breakfast this morning anyway. I've got a busy day ahead and I want to get an early start. I'll see you this evening.'

'Oh, I forgot to tell you,' Kira said as she sat up. 'I'll be late home. One of the nurses is getting married on Saturday and I've been asked to her hen-party.'

'I'll get something to eat, then, before I get home,' Glenn said. 'What time do you expect to be in?'

'I shouldn't think I'll be that late. Soon after ten, I expect.'

'Fine,' Glenn agreed. 'Well, have a good time.'

He leant over the bed and kissed her lightly on the lips before leaving the room. For a while she lay back, perfectly content in the bed's warmth, curiously reluctant to get up. Then, hearing the sound of the front door, she got out of bed and blew Glenn a kiss from the window as he glanced up before opening the car door. He smiled at her, that attractive, knowing smile that made it seem as if they communicated at a level deeper than words. They hadn't made love last night but she knew that this morning, if he hadn't been in such a rush, they would have made up for the omission.

Glenn's Mercedes swung out of the drive and Kira moved away from the window before suddenly clamping her hand over her mouth and rushing to the bathroom. She clutched the washbasin as dizziness and nausea swept over her. Trembling, she stayed there till the sickening feeling subsided a little. She sat down shakily on the edge of the bath. What on earth was wrong with her? And then suddenly she guessed with blinding certainty. She and Glenn had taken no precautions when they'd made love. She must be pregnant. She put a hand on her stomach, unable to believe that such a miracle could have happened to her.

She'd had such difficulty in conceiving it didn't seem possible that she could now be carrying Glenn's child. Fighting a renewed wave of nausea, she pulled on her wrap and hurried downstairs to check her diary. She turned the pages, emotion bringing a rush of colour to her face as she counted the weeks and realised she was overdue. A sense of complete incredulous elation enfolded her, a feeling of wonder all the more intense because she had been so certain she would never fall pregnant. Glenn's baby. She repeated the words, checked her diary again as though suddenly afraid she might be mistaken. And then she smiled.

Her heart raced a little as she thought of telling

Glenn. She was so excited, she couldn't wait to share the news with him. And then caution sobered her. She spread a protective hand over her stomach. She wanted to be certain before she told him, absolutely certain. She decided she'd wait till she'd been to the doctor.

She wouldn't have believed it was possible to feel so euphoric and so sick at the same time. She made herself a cup of tea and forced herself to nibble some crispbread—sensible hospital training, she thought, amused at herself, though breakfast did make her feel less queasy.

It was not till she was on her way to work that it occurred to her to speculate as to which occasion she had actually conceived. Quite possibly it was the night Glenn had come back from the accounting institute's long weekend. She felt a stab of pain as the thought reminded her of Clare. Then certainty eased it away. Whatever there was, or had been, between him and Clare, *she* was carrying his child. Perhaps this was the final element that would make their marriage complete. She wasn't afraid of Clare any more. She knew she could fight her and win. Glenn hadn't put any pressure on her by mentioning children since they'd been married, but she knew from the way he treated Heather that he must be hoping for some of his own.

She rang her own doctor from the hospital to make an appointment for the following day. It was a temptation afterwards to pick the phone up again and call Glenn, not because she had changed her mind about telling him, but she expected he'd be busy and, in any case, they'd be together this evening. She wished suddenly she hadn't got to stay to the party. She wanted to be with Glenn.

As it was, she compromised by not staying too long. It was a large party held in the nurses' hostel and it was quite easy to slip away. The throb of music followed her from the building as she walked to her car. She started the Rover's engine and pulled away.

With the roads quiet and empty she had a quick drive home. She was about to turn into their circular drive when she noticed a red Mazda parked on the road outside the house. She glanced at the number-plate, wondering which of their friends had called round, but the car wasn't familiar.

At that moment the front door opened and for an instant Clare and Glenn stood silhouetted against the light. There was something about the way they were standing, their shadows fused together, that spoke irrefutably of a man and a woman with things shared between them. Then Clare stepped out into the porch. Even in Kira's cold disbelief and anger she noticed the cut-away halterneck dress Clare was wearing, the high-healed Italian sandals. She moved as though underneath the dress she was naked, and Kira's hands tightened on the steering wheel as she brought the car to a halt in the drive.

The glare of the Rover's headlamps caught Clare in their white beam. She half turned and put a hand up in acknowledgement to Kira before running towards her car, getting in and roaring away.

The casualness of the gesture was the final goad. In blazing anger Kira stormed into the house to confront Glenn. He was standing waiting for her as she approached in outraged fury.

'So,' she began in a choked voice. 'I can't even be out of the house for one evening before you bring your damned mistress round here. In *our* house,' she said, pain tearing at her and making her words all the more venemous. 'Our house! You bastard! How could you do this to me?'

She didn't get any further. Glenn grabbed hold of her angrily by the arm. He swung her inside, pushing the door shut with one hand and pinioning her against the wall with the other.

'Now, what the hell is this about?' he demanded savagely.

'What's it about?' she repeated, her voice rising within a notch of breaking. 'It's about your not being any different from Stuart . . .'

'I've heard enough of this,' Glenn snarled, his eyes burning her.

'Well, you have a lot in common. He couldn't be faithful to me either.'

'My God!' Glenn exclaimed wrathfully. 'What do you think I've been doing here with Clare this evening? You surely don't imagine we've been making love on the floor.'

'You disgust me,' she sobbed, the words torn from her. 'No, undoubtedly you had more finesse that that. I expect you made use of the bedroom.'

She gasped as he grabbed hold of her by the shoulders with both hands and, for a frightening instant, she thought he was going to shake her senseless.

'I can't believe I'm hearing this.' Fury and incredulity blazed in his blue eyes. 'You see someone I work with leaving the house and you assume I've been to bed with her. What on earth's wrong with you.?'

'So there's nothing between the two of you?' Kira said, her voice loaded with derision.

'No! Nothing!' he fired back at her.

'You *liar*!' she hissed. 'You despicable liar!'

His eyes hardened. He jerked her away from the wall, taking her like a prisoner under guard into the lounge where he pushed her roughly into an armchair. Standing over her, he said, his voice lowered threatening forcefulness, 'You'd better start giving me some explanations, Kira.'

'Don't you dare play the wronged party with me!' she said, her voice tight with emotion as she stumbled to her feet and backed away from him. 'You thought you were so clever, didn't you? So damned clever you could even have Clare at the house and I'd never suspect. Well, you were wrong because I *know*! I saw you with her in your room at the institute's headquarters. I heard you telling her how unforgettable you'd found her . . .'

She couldn't go on. Her voice broke, but her eyes still defied his, filled with bitterness and accusation.

'You *heard what*?' he asked in angry incomprehension.

'I not only heard,' she said shakenly. 'I *saw*. The two of you together. She was in your arms.'

Clarity suddenly sharpened Glenn's shrewd blue eyes. With curbed exasperation he began, 'You've put two and two together and come up with five.

'I know what I saw!' she said heatedly.

'What you saw was Clare in tears and me trying to make her feel better, not because I'd slept with her, but because I hadn't. She'd wanted me to, and then the morning after felt mortified because she'd made it clear she was so available.'

Kira stared at him, the forcefulness of his words somehow communicating to her that he was telling the truth.

'There is nothing between me and Clare,' he went on, his voice roughened with anger. 'We were friends at university, a happy, reasonably platonic friendship that never ended in bed. After she married I didn't see her for years. Then she applied for a job with the firm and I took her on because she's a first-class accountant. She's only recently divorced from her husband and she feels insecure. She needed to restore her self-esteem and because of it she came to my room that night. But nothing happened. I turned her down. I didn't want her. I've never wanted any woman but you. What you overheard the next morning was my rather clumsy attempt to make her feel better after she'd broken down in tears and said how cheap she felt.'

His tirade stopped and there was an uneasy, throbbing silence while Kira still stared at him, her face still pale and shocked.

'Then why was she here tonight?' she whispered.

From the look that crossed his face at her question she had the strong impression he'd have like to have resorted to violence.

'Because she went for a job interview with another company today. She called round to say she'd got the job and she's leaving the firm. After the way she offered herself to me she's been awkward with me ever since.'

Kira gave a little convulsive catch of breath as she suppressed tears of relief. She crossed over to the sofa and sat down weakly.

'I'm sorry,' she began inadequately in a voice that didn't sound like her own. 'I thought . . . I thought she was your mistress.'

'You have a very high opinion of me,' Glenn said bitingly.

Her head went up and she glared at him for an instant.

'You might think how it looked to me when I saw you together,' she retaliated.

'I *am* thinking of how it looked,' he said. 'And I'm also thinking of how you chose to interpret it in the worst possible way.'

'I've said I'm sorry,' she said, conscious of pain tightening round her heart. He'd said he'd never slept with Clare and she believed him. So what was still wrong between them? She saw that his face was set hard and she asked in desperation, 'What *more* do you want me to say?'

'Something that will make me damned well understand you,' he said harshly, about to walk out of the room.

She got swiftly to her feet.

'Glenn . . .' she began.

He halted and then turned slowly back to face her, his eyes angry and bitter. She noted the animal grace and power in his build, and she wanted nothing more than to go blindly into his arms and have him kiss her. But he made no move towards her and, as the silence between them lengthened, she said with a surge of hostility, 'Maybe you would understand me if you tried a little harder.'

She saw but without comprehending it that she had brought their conversation back to some kind of flash point of final resolution.

'Try harder!' Glenn repeated, snatching hold of her. 'My God, Kira, I've been to hell and back trying to work you out. And I'm still no closer than I was before. You've just accused me of sleeping with Clare. You've told me the conclusion you jumped to when you saw us together, and yet I'm supposed to believe that after that, you were here waiting for me when I got back. You said in the car park that day you were leaving me. Now I see why. What I don't see is what made you change your mind.'

'I would have thought it was obvious,' she said, matching his wrath.

'Well, spell it out, as I seem to be being a little slow,' he said furiously, biting sarcasm in his voice. 'It's strange to think you could be so eager and responsive that night if you really believed I'd spent the weekend with my mistress. Just what did make you change your mind about leaving me?'

'Because I *love you*,' she stormed, the words almost wrenched from her.

The violence went out of the hands that still gripped her. And then, after a long silence, his eyes dark and searching, he said in a strangely intense voice, 'I thought I'd never hear you say it.'

Suddenly she knew why he'd been so watchful with her, understood the overwhelming demand with which he made love to her, as though he meant her to drown in her longing for him. She couldn't speak. She'd thought that night when she'd given herself to him so completely that her confession of love had gone beyond words. And then, afterwards, her uncertainty about whether he was still having an affair with Clare had made her too insecure to say the words. The moment was emblazoned with sudden understanding, and without thought she went into his arms, pressing her body tightly against his, her fingers smoothing the hair at the nape of his neck as, in a breathless whisper, she made the admission again and again.

When at last he released her a little, she looked up at him with smoky, inviting eyes, letting him see her desire and her love. He breathed her name raggedly before bending his head and kissing her with passion laced with tenderness. He kissed her long and deeply, making a helpless, melting pleasure race through her. When finally he raised his head his eyes met hers, and Kira coloured slightly as the flash of knowledge swept between them of the feverish ecstasy that would come later in bed.

Glenn drew her on to the sofa, his mouth travelling to her throat, pressing small kisses on her skin.

'I never guessed you were jealous of Clare,' he murmured. 'I suppose it was because I never loved her.' Amusement came into his voice as he added, 'I should have known you were the intense, jealous type.'

She slid her fingers into his dark hair, a shade breathless with the pleasure of his touch, and the heady knowledge that he loved and wanted her. Her eyes were soft with warm answering laughter as she said, recognising at last the sexual attraction his sense of humour had always had for her, 'Aren't we all jealous for the things we love?'

Glenn traced a caressing hand along the line of her face, the mood altering to intensity again as he murmured, 'You're a complicated lady, but there's a magnetism between us, Kira, that brooks no interference, some elemental force pulling us together.'

'It's lucky for Clare she got in her car and drove off when she did, or she'd certainly have felt some elemental force,' Kira said with a husky little laugh.

She felt the shake of mirth in Glenn's body as he pulled her tightly against him, and she laughed with him, feeling suddenly carefree and very secure. Kissing him lightly on the lips she drew away and said, 'Let's have a drink before we turn in.'

'OK,' he agreed. 'What shall it be?'

'I'd like tea.'

'Then, while you make it, I'll put your car in the garage,' he said.

She went through into the kitchen to make a pot of tea. She put the kettle on the gas and crossed to the cupboard to get the cups. Then she paused as on the table she saw a British Airways travel folder.

'What's this?' she asked, picking it up and turning to Glenn as she heard him come into the kitchen.

'Our tickets for our flight to Toronto,' he said, linking his arms lightly round her waist, amusement and love in his eyes as he saw delight come into her face.

'You mean we're going to Canada, so that Heather can travel home with us?'

'That's right,' he confirmed. 'I thought we'd have a week by ourselves to do some sightseeing and then a week with Heather as well before coming home as a family.'

The word made her think of the child she was carrying and she almost told him. But instead, wanting to be sure, she wound her arms round his neck and whispered, her voice unsteady with emotion, 'Glenn, I love you so very much.'

When he made love to her that night it was with a demanding passionate insistence that left them both overwhelmed. She curled against him, lulled to a sensual peace that made her glory in her womanly abandon.

In the darkness Glenn said softly, 'No tears tonight.'

'Why should there be?' she murmured.

'I was getting used to your crying after we'd made love,' he said, and there was something in his voice that made her ask,

'Does it spoil it for you that I'm not crying?'

He gave a ragged laugh. 'God, no!'

'What, then?' she asked, bewildered.

He shifted so that he could look down at her, smoothing her hair away from her face with a hand that was both possessive and tender.

'Can't you imagine what I thought when I used to feel you shaking with sobs beside me? The first time it happened I was moved beyond words because I thought that for some reason you believed I didn't love you and you needed reassurance. But then, when it went on, I could only believe you were thinking of Stuart.'

His voice was a shade rough, and intuitively she knew he was still wondering how tied she was to Stuart's memory.

'The tears were because of Clare,' she whispered. 'Only that. I promise you.'

She knew that he needed to hear more. She had been reticent with him for so long, denying her feelings, that she couldn't expect him to believe immediately how deeply she loved him. Running her hand tenderly over his chest she went on, 'I don't know precisely when I fell in love with you. Even that night after I slept with you before we were married, I wouldn't admit how much you meant to me. I tried to think of it as some kind of madness. With Stuart I'd learned what it meant to love someone and not be loved in return. It was a torment I couldn't go through again.'

'You don't have to tell me anything about that kind of hell,' he said quietly.

She glanced up at him and whispered, 'You loved me right from the beginning, didn't you? And I never guessed.'

'I came to understand that in the end. But for a time I thought you were on some kind of power trip, that you knew the fascination you had for me, and that was why after Stuart was dead I got such a mixture of fire and ice from you. Even when I made love to you I didn't realise how confused you were, how unawakened, even though you'd been married.' A note of wry humour came into his voice as he said, 'I'd done such a first-class job of making you dislike me,'

'And then you did a similarly first-class job of making me love you,' she said with a smile. She lapsed into silence for a while and then said quietly, 'If I'd known Stuart was cheating on me, I think I'd have left him. With you, when I believed you'd slept with Clare, I knew I had to fight tooth and nail to save our marriage.'

'Kira, don't,' he said gently. 'I know you loved Stuart. I don't begrudge him that—not any more.'

'It's important that I say it. You're right, I did love Stuart, but what we have is so much stronger. Glenn, I feel so ashamed that I was so hateful to you for so long.'

'No,' he whispered tenderly, kissing her temple. 'It wasn't your fault. I'd established the enmity between us. Right from the beginning I felt it was me you should have married, not Stuart. But he was my partner and I owed him the loyalty of not trying to seduce his wife. What I didn't reckon on was that every day I'd find it harder to deal with the way I felt about you. You were in my thoughts all the time.

'If it had been possible I'd have moved away to get free from the magnetic pull I felt when I was near you. But Stuart was so anxious I shouldn't pull out of the firm because of the financial implications, I realised if I insisted he'd start to look for reasons for why I wanted to break up the partnership. And then I found out . . .'

He checked what he'd been going to say and Kira murmured, 'You don't have to shield me any more, Glenn. I can face up to the fact now that Stuart was unfaithful to me.'

'Stuart just wasn't the monogamous type,' Glenn said. 'I was so furious when I realised what was going on I didn't know what to do—whether to clear out, or to stick around in case you needed me.'

'I *do* need you,' she said, a catch in her voice. She had done everything she could to shatter their relationship in her blindness and distrust, but through it all he'd never stopped loving her. Neither had he forfeited his integrity. Mingled with her love was a sudden respect for his sense of honour and his strength. Kissing him, she whispered, 'I've been such a fool to make you wait so long to hear me say how much I love you.'

'I'd have waited for ever,' Glen said, taking her hand in his.

Bending his head, he pressed the palm to his lips and then traced the vein on her wrist with his tongue. A quicksilver quiver of excitement went through her, for she was familiar enough now with the pattern of their lovemaking to know that this was the slow beginning of a lingering seduction of her senses by him.

He encircled her in his arms, drawing her more tightly against his strong male body and holding her close for a moment before brushing her hair with his lips and surprising her by saying, 'Kira, when we get back from Canada I want you to have those medical tests you spoke of. I know you said they were an emotional ordeal, and I understand that. But I know how badly you want a child, and I want us to share that together.'

She raised her head to look at him, her vision misting with emotional tears.

'I'll give you all the love and support I can,' Glenn told her, his voice gentle, yet with a force of purpose in it. 'Believe me. I . . .'

She put trembling fingers against his lips, her desire to be absolutely certain swamped by her need to share with him the fact that she believed she was already carrying his child.

'I don't think I'm going to need the tests,' she said softly.

He looked at her sharply, and she had the joy of seeing comprehension come gradually into his blue eyes. Laughing, she confirmed, 'I think I'm pregnant. In fact, I'm almost sure.'

'Darling . . . sweetheart . . .'

She was amazed at the emotion in his voice and cut across him, 'I said, *almost* sure.'

'That's good enough for me. When are you seeing the doctor? Kira, this is wonderful! How long have you known?'

He swept her into his arms, kissing her intensely. When their lips at last parted she said, laughing, 'Give me a chance to answer! I realised this morning, and I'm seeing the doctor tomorrow. Oh, Glenn, you don't know what this means to me, how happy the thought of our having a baby makes me. I meant not to tell you until I was sure, but I just couldn't keep it to myself any longer. I only hope and pray the doctor confirms I'm right.'

'We could always "make assurance double sure",' Glenn suggested, desire and laughter in his voice as his hands travelled in an arousing caress over the curves of her body.

'You promised me I'd be pregnant before the year

was out, do you remember?' she whispered enticingly as she slid her fingers down his spine, feeling his shudder of pleasure under her sensuous fingers.

'You witch,' he murmured, his hand gentle and shatteringly erotic as he stroked her breast. 'You're sheer magic, Kira, magic in every way—enchantment for a lifetime.'

Then, tantalisingly and slowly, he drew them deep into the vortex of spinning desire, until they reached a union so complete and dazzlingly beautiful that time and place were lost in the mystery of their love.

Harlequin Presents

Coming Next Month

1223 DEEP HARBOUR Sally Cook
Lucy had enjoyed the summer with her aunt's family in Minorca until strange things started to happen. Unafraid, she decides to investigate, only to discover that everything seems to lead back to a mysterious man in one of the villas.

1224 ONE HOUR OF MAGIC Melinda Cross
Robert Chesterfield had been full of light and laughter, while Daniel, his brother, had been so dark and brooding. Now, with Robert dead and Daniel providing her with a home and a job, Holly wonders how she can live with someone who hated the man she loved.

1225 LOVEKNOT Catherine George
Sophie's life had always been planned by those around her, particularly her father and brothers. Now everything is changing, and Sophie plans to change, too. Then why is it so difficult to leave her aloof, unapproachable boss, nicknamed Alexander the Great?

1226 REMEMBER TOMORROW Pamela Hatton
Powerful, arrogant Ross Tyler is fighting painful injuries as well as the belief that Cassie had deserted him after the car crash. When they finally chance to meet, Ross discovers that Cassie didn't even know he was alive.

1227 THE LOVING GIFT Carole Mortimer
David Kendrick falls in love with Jade at first sight—but that doesn't mean she has to put up with his impulsive pursuit. He might be charming, but since she's still running away from a hurtful past, surely it's better not to start anything?

1228 DON'T ASK WHY Annabel Murray
Why is the stranger in the astrakhan coat following her husband? Determined to find out, Giana's search soon leads her to greater confusion and a life of lies and subterfuge in the employ of the semireclusive Breid Winterton.

1229 MAN WITHOUT A PAST Valerie Parv
"Don't love me, Gaelle," Dan warns her, "for your own sake." But it is already far too late to tell her that. And neither of them can foresee just how impossible their love is....

1230 UNWILLING HEART Emma Richmond
O'Malley coped with being buried alive in an earthquake in Turkey—and having to dig her way out. But being kidnapped by a mysterious Frenchman, whom she knows only as Paget, is another matter entirely!

Available in December wherever paperback books are sold, or through Harlequin Reader Service:

In the U.S.
901 Fuhrmann Blvd.
P.O. Box 1397
Buffalo, N.Y. 14240-1397

In Canada
P.O. Box 603
Fort Erie, Ontario
L2A 5X3

CHRISTMAS IS FOR KIDS

Spend this holiday season with nine very special children. Children whose wishes come true at the magical time of Christmas.

Read American Romance's CHRISTMAS IS FOR KIDS—heartwarming holiday stories in which children bring together four couples who fall in love. Meet:

Frank, Dorcas, Kathy, Candy and Nicky—They become friends at St. Christopher's orphanage, but they really want to be adopted and become part of a real family, in #321 *A Carol Christmas* by Muriel Jensen.

Patty—She's a ten-year-old certified genius, but she wants what every little girl wishes for: a daddy of her own, in #322 *Mrs. Scrooge* by Barbara Bretton.

Amy and Flash—Their mom is about to deliver their newest sibling any day, but Christmas just isn't the same now—not without their dad. More than anything they want their family reunited for Christmas, in #323 *Dear Santa* by Margaret St. George.

Spencer—Living with his dad and grandpa in an all-male household has its advantages, but Spence wants Santa to bring him a mommy to love, in #324 *The Best Gift of All* by Andrea Davidson.

These children will win your hearts as they entice—and matchmake—the adults into a true romance. This holiday, invite them—and the four couples they bring together—into your home.

Look for all four CHRISTMAS IS FOR KIDS books coming in December from Harlequin American Romance. And happy holidays!

**A distinctive romance chosen
to salute Penny Jordan fans**

Harlequin Presents...

PENNY JORDAN

lovers touch

Harlequin is pleased to present this special
Penny Jordan title guaranteed to capture
your heart and enchant you as only Penny
Jordan can. *Lovers Touch* is specially selected
to receive the November Award of Excellence,
an honor reserved for your favorite authors.

Look for Harlequin Presents #1216,
Lovers Touch, and the special Award
of Excellence seal of approval
wherever Harlequin books
are sold.

AE-LT-1

Have You Ever Wondered If You Could Write A Harlequin Novel?

Here's great news—Harlequin is offering a series of cassette tapes to help you do just that. Written by Harlequin editors, these tapes give practical advice on how to make your characters—and your story—come alive. There's a tape for each contemporary romance series Harlequin publishes.

Mail order only

All sales final
